EDGAR ALLAN POE'S
TALES OF MYSTERY

Graphic Classics® Volume Twenty-One

2011

Edited by Tom Pomplun

EUREKA PRODUCTIONS

8778 Oak Grove Road, Mount Horeb, Wisconsin 53572

www.graphicclassics.com

ILLUSTRATION ©2006 SKOT OLSEN

ALONE

by Edgar Allan Poe
illustrated by Maxon Crumb

From childhood's hour I have not been
As others were—I have not seen
As others saw—I could not bring
My passions from a common spring—
From the same source I have not taken
My sorrow—I could not awaken
My heart to joy at the same tone—
And all I lov'd—I lov'd alone—
Then—in my childhood—in the dawn
Of a most stormy life—was drawn
From ev'ry depth of good and ill
The mystery which binds me still—
From the torrent, or the fountain—
From the red cliff of the mountain—
From the sun that 'round me roll'd
In its autumn tint of gold—
From the lightning in the sky
As it pass'd me flying by—
From the thunder, and the storm—
And the cloud that took the form
(When the rest of Heaven was blue)
Of a demon in my view.

CONTENTS

EDGAR ALLAN POE'S
TALES OF MYSTERY

Graphic Classics® Volume Twenty-One

ILLUSTRATION ©2011 BRAD TEARE

Cover illustration by Michael Manning / Back cover illustration by Stan Shaw
Additional illustrations by Skot Olsen and Brad Teare

Edgar Allan Poe's Tales of Mystery: Graphic Classics Volume Twenty-One / ISBN 978-0-9825630-2-1 is published by Eureka Productions. Price US $17.95, CAN $22.50. Available from Eureka Productions, 8778 Oak Grove Road, Mount Horeb, WI 53572. Tom Pomplun, designer and publisher, tom@graphicclassics.com. Eileen Fitzgerald, editorial assistant. Compilation and all original works ©2011 Eureka Productions. Graphic Classics is a registered trademark of Eureka Productions. For ordering information and previews of upcoming volumes visit the Graphic Classics website at http://www.graphicclassics.com. Printed in USA.

The Murders in the Rue Morgue

by **Edgar Allan Poe**
adapted by **Antonella Caputo**
illustrated by **Reno Maniquis**

The analytical power should not be confounded with simple ingenuity. Between them exists a difference far greater than that between fancy and imagination, but they are analogous. The ingenious is always fanciful, and the truly imaginative never otherwise than analytic.

Residing in Paris during the spring of 1882, I became acquainted with a Monsieur Auguste Dupin.

This young gentleman was of an excellent family, but had been reduced to such poverty that his character had succumbed beneath it.

He managed, by means of a rigorous economy, to procure the necessities of life.

BONJOUR, DUPIN! HAVE A LOOK AT THIS. I NEVER THOUGHT I WOULD FIND THIS BOOK!

Books were his sole luxuries. Our first meeting was at an obscure library in the Rue Montmartre. After that, we saw each other again and again.

AH! IT IS A TREASURE, INDEED!

I felt my soul enkindled by the freshness of his imagination, and we agreed to live together during my stay in the city.

I BELIEVE I KNOW JUST THE HOUSE TO SUIT US.

I FEEL WE ARE KINDRED SPIRITS, MON AMI.

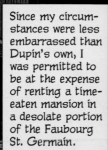

Since my circumstances were less embarrassed than Dupin's own, I was permitted to be at the expense of renting a time-eaten mansion in a desolate portion of the Faubourg St. Germain.

It was a freak of fancy in my friend to be enamoured of the night. At the first dawn of the morning we closed the shutters and lighted a couple of tapers.

We busied our souls in reading, writing or conversing until warned by the clock of the advent of the true darkness.

Then we sallied forth into the streets, seeking that mental excitement which quiet observation can afford.

We were strolling one night, when Dupin broke forth with these words:

HE IS A VERY LITTLE FELLOW, THAT'S TRUE, AND WOULD BE BETTER FOR THE THEATRE DES VARIETIES.

DUPIN, THIS IS BEYOND MY COMPREHENSION! HOW WAS IT POSSIBLE YOU SHOULD KNOW I WAS THINKING OF?

I could not help admiring the analytic ability in Dupin. He boasted to me that most men wore windows in their bosoms, and was wont to follow up such assertions by direct proofs of his intimate knowledge of myself.

CHANTILLY? YOU WERE REMARKING TO YOURSELF THAT HIS DIMINUTIVE FIGURE UNFITTED HIM FOR TRAGEDY.

This was precisely the subject of my reflection. Chantilly was once a cobbler who attempted the role of Xerxes and had been notoriously mocked for his pains.

BOOOO!

BOOOO...!!

OFF! OFF!

TELL ME THE METHOD BY WHICH YOU HAVE BEEN ENABLED TO FATHOM MY SOUL IN THIS MATTER!

IT WAS THE FRUITERER WHO BROUGHT YOU TO THE CONCLUSION THAT THE COBBLER WAS NOT OF SUFFICIENT HEIGHT FOR XERXES.

THE FRUITERER! I KNOW NO FRUITERER WHOMSOEVER!

THE MAN WHO RAN UP AGAINST YOU AS WE ENTERED THE STREET...

...IT MAY HAVE BEEN FIFTEEN MINUTES AGO.

I now remembered a fruiterer who had bumped into me. But what this had to do with Chantilly I could not understand.

I WILL EXPLAIN. WE WILL RETRACE THE COURSE OF YOUR MEDITATIONS.

THE CHAIN RUNS: CHANTILLY, ORION, EPICURUS, STEREOTOMY, THE STREET STONES, THE FRUITERER.

HEY, WATCH OUT!

SORRY, SIR!

"You slipped and slightly strained your ankle."

OUCH!

"You then kept your eye upon the pavement, until we reached a little alley..."

"As we crossed into this street a fruiterer, brushing quickly past us, pushed you into a pile of paving stones."

"Here your countenance brightened, and I heard you murmur..."

STEREOTOMY...

"...a term referring to the species of stonework you were observing."

"Stereotomy brought you to think of the theories of Epicurus. We discussed not long ago how the vague guesses of that noble Greek have been confirmed in recent cosmogony."

"Yesterday's newspaper alluded to the cobbler's change of name upon taking the stage, quoting the line: *Perdidit antiquum litera prima sonum*, which referred to *Orion*, formerly written '*Urion*'."

IT WAS CLEAR, THEREFORE, THAT YOU WOULD COMBINE THE IDEAS OF ORION AND CHANTILLY.

YOU HAD BEEN STOOPING IN YOUR GAIT, AND I SAW YOU DRAW YOURSELF UP TO YOUR FULL HEIGHT...

...THEN I WAS SURE THAT YOU WERE REFLECTING UPON THE SMALL FIGURE OF CHANTILLY!

AND IT WAS THEN *YOU* MADE YOUR REMARK THAT CHANTILLY WAS A VERY LITTLE FELLOW, AND HE WOULD DO BETTER AT THE THEATRE DES VARIETES!

Not long after this, we were looking over the *Gazette des Tribunaux* when a paragraph arrested our attention:

"THIS MORNING ABOUT THREE O'CLOCK, THE INHABITANTS OF THE QUARTIER ST. ROCH WERE AROUSED FROM SLEEP BY A SERIES OF TERRIFIC SHRIEKS, ISSUING FROM THE FOURTH STORY OF A HOUSE IN THE RUE MORGUE..."

"...KNOWN TO BE IN THE SOLE OCCUPANCY OF MADAME L'ESPANAYE AND HER DAUGHTER CAMILLE..."

"THE GATEWAY WAS BROKEN IN, AND SOME OF THE NEIGHBORS ENTERED, ACCOMPANIED BY TWO GENDARMES. BY THIS TIME THE CRIES HAD CEASED..."

GRAFTBLE
DIABLE!
AARRHHHUBLE
CRASHTABLY
SCHRIIETED
MON DIEU!!
SACRE!

"Two or more voices were distinguished from above. As the second landing was reached, these sounds also had ceased. All remained quiet as the party hurried up the stairs."

"The apartment was in the wildest disorder. Of Madame L'Espanaye, no traces were seen."

THE SAFE IS UNLOCKED, BUT IT CONTAINS ONLY LETTERS.

THESE ARE GOLDEN NAPOLEONS!

"An unusual quantity of soot being observed in the fireplace, a search was made of the chimney, and the corpse of the daughter was discovered."

"Many excoriations were perceived, and upon the throat, bruises, as if the deceased had been throttled to death."

"AFTER AN INVESTIGATION OF THE HOUSE, THE PARTY MADE ITS WAY INTO A SMALL PAVED YARD IN THE REAR OF THE BUILDING..."

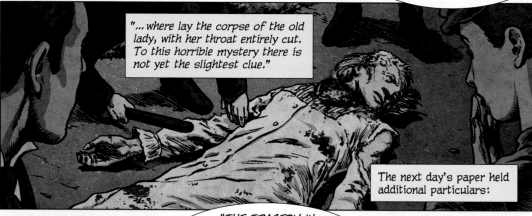

"...where lay the corpse of the old lady, with her throat entirely cut. To this horrible mystery there is not yet the slightest clue."

The next day's paper held additional particulars:

"THE TRAGEDY IN THE RUE MORGUE — MANY INDIVIDUALS HAVE BEEN EXAMINED IN RELATION TO THIS FRIGHTFUL AFFAIR WE GIVE BELOW ALL THE MATERIAL TESTIMONY SOLICITED."

HAVE YOU SEEN ANYONE ELSE IN THE BUILDING?

NO, I NEVER MET ANYONE. THEY HAD NO SERVANT IN EMPLOY.

"Pauline Duborg, laundress: She knew both the deceased, having washed for them."

"Pierre Moreau, tobacconist: He had been selling tobacco and snuff to Madame L. for more than six years."

WERE YOU AWARE OF THE MEANS BY WHICH THEY LIVED?

THE HOUSE WAS THE PROPERTY OF MADAME L. THE TWO LIVED AN EXCEEDINGLY RETIRED LIFE.

DID ANYONE ELSE FREQUENT THE HOUSE?

IT SAYS, "NO ONE WAS SPOKEN OF AS VISITING THE HOUSE."

"THE SHUTTERS OF THE FRONT WINDOWS WERE SELDOM OPENED..."

"...THOSE AT THE REAR WERE ALWAYS CLOSED, WITH THE EXCEPTION OF THE LARGE BACK ROOM, FOURTH STORY."

THE SHRIEKS SUDDENLY CEASED, THEN I COULD DISTINGUISH THE WORDS "SACRE" AND "DIABLE."

YOU SAID THE OTHER VOICE WAS THAT OF A FOREIGNER?

YES, SIR. I BELIEVE THE LANGUAGE TO BE SPANISH.

"Isidore Muset, Gendarme: He was called to the house about three in the morning."

"Henri Duval, a neighbor: He was sure that the second voice was not that of either deceased."

I HEARD A SHRILL VOICE; I AM CONVINCED BY THE INTONATION THAT THE SPEAKER WAS ITALIAN.

HE SAYS HE WAS PASSING BY WHEN HE HEARD THE SHRIEKS.

HE IS CERTAIN ONE VOICE WAS OF A FRENCH MAN.

"Odenheimer, restaurateur and native of Amsterdam: As he does not speak French, he was examined through an interpreter."

11

"Jules Mignaud, banker of the firm Mignaud et Fils:"

ADOLPHE WILL ESCORT YOU TO YOUR HOME, FOR SECURITY.

IT IS VERY KIND OF YOU, MONSIEUR MIGNAUD.

"The third day before her death Madame L'Esplanaye took out the sum of 4000 francs."

"Adolphe Le Bon, bank clerk: He accompanied Madame to her residence. Mademoiselle L. appeared and took from his hands the bag..."

"...He then bowed and departed. He did not see any person in the street at the time."

"William Bird, tailor: He was one of the party who entered the house. He is English. He heard two voices. The gruff one was that of a Frenchman. The shrill voice he thought that of a German."

"FOUR OF THE ABOVE-NAMED WITNESSES DEPOSED THAT THE DOOR OF THE CHAMBER IN WHICH WAS FOUND THE BODY OF MADEMOISELLE L. WAS LOCKED ON THE INSIDE..."

"Everything was silent. Upon forcing the door, no person was seen."

"The windows were down and firmly fastened."

"The door leading from the back room to the passage was locked, with the key inside."

"THERE WAS NOT AN INCH OF THE HOUSE WHICH WAS NOT CAREFULLY SEARCHED. ALFONZO GARCIO, UNDERTAKER, DEPOSES..."

I RESIDE IN THE RUE MORGUE. I COME FROM SPAIN.

DID YOU HEAR ANYTHING WHEN YOU ENTERED THE HOUSE?

SI, SENOR. I HEARD THE VOICE OF AN ENGLISHMAN. I DON'T UNDERSTAND ENGLISH, BUT I KNOW THE SOUND.

"Alberto Montani, an Italian confectioner:"

THE GRUFF VOICE WAS THAT OF A FRENCHMAN.

THE OTHER, I AM SURE, WAS THE VOICE OF A RUSSIAN.

THE CHIMNEYS WERE ALL TOO NARROW TO ADMIT THE PASSAGE OF A HUMAN BEING. THESE BRUSHES WERE PASSED THROUGH EVERY FLUE IN THE HOUSE.

THE BODY OF MADEMOISELLE L. WAS SO FIRMLY WEDGED IN THE CHIMNEY THAT IT COULD NOT BE GOT DOWN UNTIL SEVERAL OF US UNITED OUR STRENGTH!

"PAUL DUMAS, PHYSICIAN, DEPOSES THAT HE WAS CALLED TO VIEW THE BODIES. THE CORPSE OF THE YOUNG LADY WAS BRUISED AND EXCORIATED..."

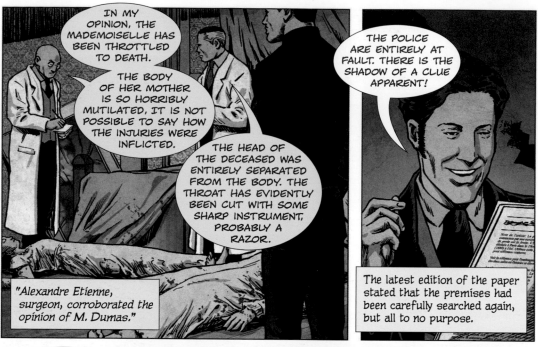

IN MY OPINION, THE MADEMOISELLE HAS BEEN THROTTLED TO DEATH.

THE BODY OF HER MOTHER IS SO HORRIBLY MUTILATED, IT IS NOT POSSIBLE TO SAY HOW THE INJURIES WERE INFLICTED.

THE HEAD OF THE DECEASED WAS ENTIRELY SEPARATED FROM THE BODY. THE THROAT HAS EVIDENTLY BEEN CUT WITH SOME SHARP INSTRUMENT, PROBABLY A RAZOR.

THE POLICE ARE ENTIRELY AT FAULT. THERE IS THE SHADOW OF A CLUE APPARENT!

"Alexandre Etienne, surgeon, corroborated the opinion of M. Dumas."

The latest edition of the paper stated that the premises had been carefully searched again, but all to no purpose.

THERE IS A POSTSCRIPT; "ADOLPHE LE BON HAS BEEN ARRESTED AND IMPRISONED..."

MAY I ASK YOUR OPINION ON THIS MATTER?

I AGREE WITH ALL PARIS THAT THIS IS AN INSOLUBLE MYSTERY.

I DON'T SEE ANY MEANS BY WHICH IT WOULD BE POSSIBLE TO TRACE THE MURDERER.

WE MUST NOT JUDGE BY THIS SHELL OF AN EXAMINATION. WE WILL GO AND SEE THE PREMISES WITH OUR OWN EYES.

I KNOW GAILLARD, THE PREFECT OF POLICE, AND WE SHALL HAVE ACCESS WITH NO DIFFICULTY.

The necessary permission was obtained and we proceeded at once to the Rue Morgue.

The Rue Morgue was a miserable thoroughfare. The house was readily found, for there were still many persons gazing up at the closed shutters. Before going in we walked up the street, and passed by the rear of the building. Then we came again to the front of the dwelling, and rang.

We showed our credentials, and were admitted by the agent in charge.

We went up the stairs, but I saw nothing beyond what had been stated in the newspaper.

Dupin scrutinised everything, not excepting the bodies of the victims.

The examination lasted until dark, when we took our departure.

I have to say that the whims of my friend were manifold. He declined all conversation on the subject of the murder until the next day...

...He then asked me suddenly:

DID YOU NOTICE ANYTHING PECULIAR AT THE SCENE?

NO, NOTHING PECULIAR. NOTHING MORE, AT LEAST, THAN WE BOTH SAW STATED IN THE PAPER.

IT APPEARS TO ME THAT THIS MYSTERY IS CONSIDERED INSOLUBLE FOR THE VERY REASON IT SHOULD BE REGARDED AS EASY OF SOLUTION.

THE POLICE ARE CONFOUNDED BY THE SEEMING ABSENCE OF MOTIVE AND THE ATROCITY OF THE MURDER. THEY HAVE CONFUSED THE UNUSUAL WITH THE ABSTRUSE.

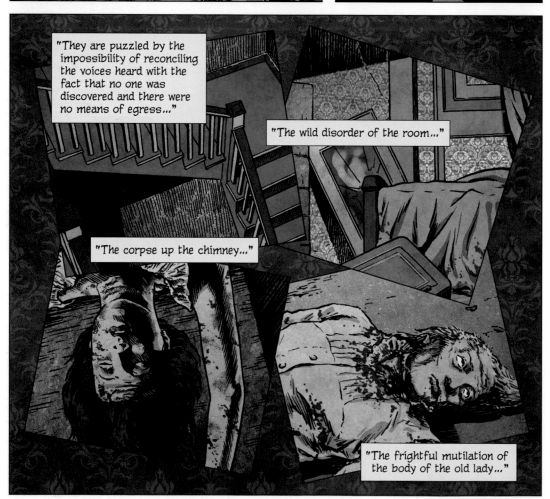

"They are puzzled by the impossibility of reconciling the voices heard with the fact that no one was discovered and there were no means of egress..."

"The wild disorder of the room..."

"The corpse up the chimney..."

"The frightful mutilation of the body of the old lady..."

16

THESE CONSIDERATIONS HAVE SUFFICED TO PARALYZE THE POLICE.

IN AN INVESTIGATION SUCH AS WE ARE NOW PURSUING, IT SHOULD NOT BE ASKED "WHAT HAS *OCCURRED*," BUT "WHAT HAS OCCURRED THAT HAS NEVER OCCURRED *BEFORE?*"

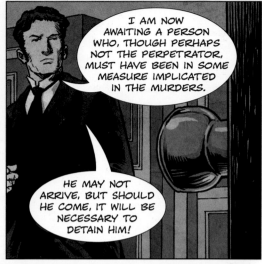

I AM NOW AWAITING A PERSON WHO, THOUGH PERHAPS NOT THE PERPETRATOR, MUST HAVE BEEN IN SOME MEASURE IMPLICATED IN THE MURDERS.

HE MAY NOT ARRIVE, BUT SHOULD HE COME, IT WILL BE NECESSARY TO DETAIN HIM!

HERE ARE PISTOLS, AND WE BOTH KNOW HOW TO USE THEM WHEN OCCASION DEMANDS THEIR USE!

THE VOICES HEARD BY THE PARTY WERE NOT THOSE OF THE WOMEN THEMSELVES. MURDER HAS BEEN COMMITTED BY SOME THIRD PARTY. AND THE VOICES OF THIS THIRD PARTY WERE THOSE HEARD IN CONTENTION. DID YOU OBSERVE ANYTHING UNUSUAL ABOUT THIS TESTIMONY?

YES; ALL THE WITNESSES AGREED THAT THE GRUFF VOICE WAS THAT OF A FRENCHMAN, BUT THERE WAS MUCH DISAGREEMENT IN REGARD TO THE SECOND VOICE.

THE PECULIARITY IS NOT THAT THEY DISAGREED, BUT THAT EACH SPOKE OF IT AS THAT OF A FOREIGNER.

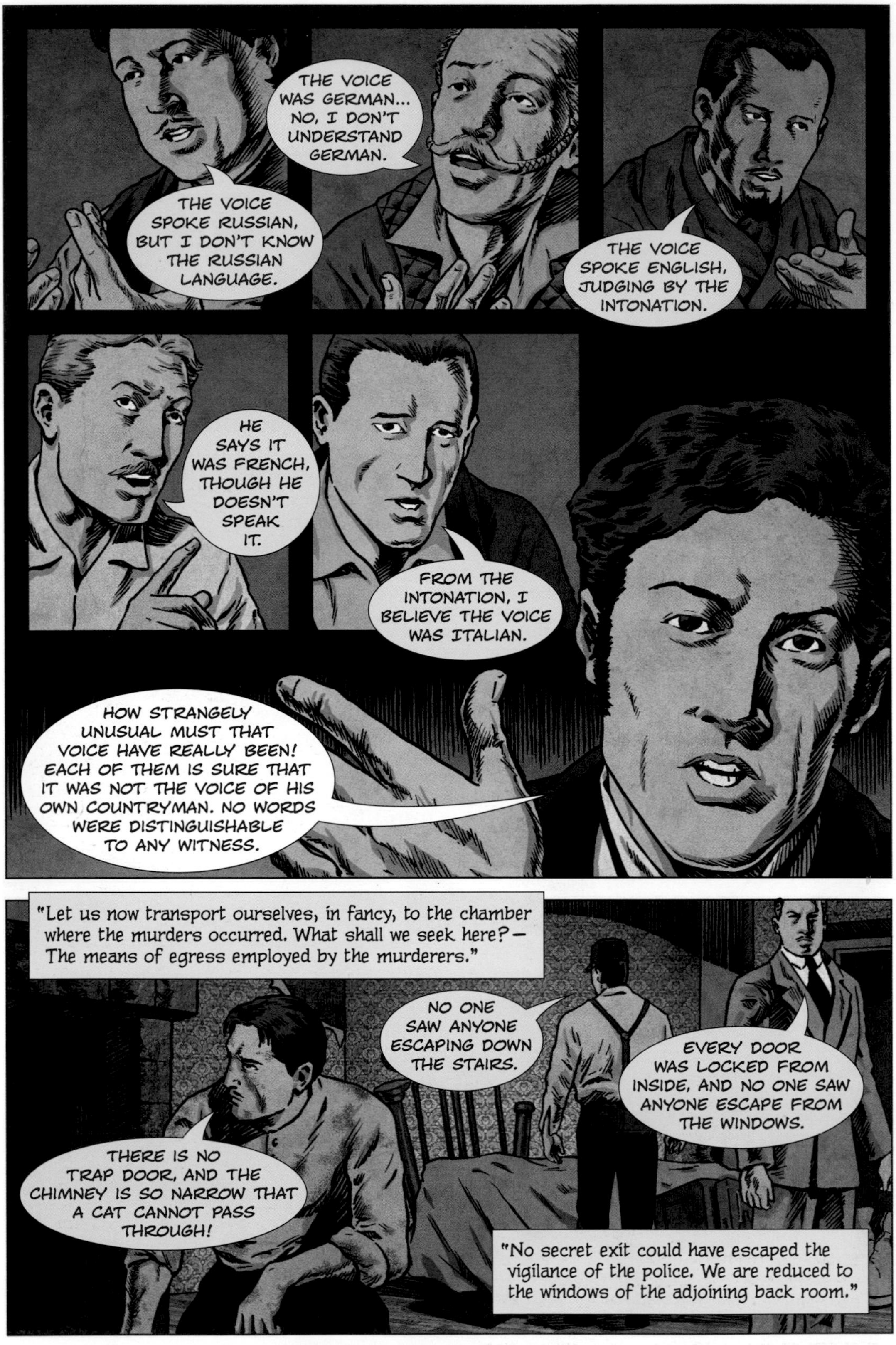
THE VOICE SPOKE RUSSIAN, BUT I DON'T KNOW THE RUSSIAN LANGUAGE.
THE VOICE WAS GERMAN... NO, I DON'T UNDERSTAND GERMAN.
THE VOICE SPOKE ENGLISH, JUDGING BY THE INTONATION.
HE SAYS IT WAS FRENCH, THOUGH HE DOESN'T SPEAK IT.
FROM THE INTONATION, I BELIEVE THE VOICE WAS ITALIAN.
HOW STRANGELY UNUSUAL MUST THAT VOICE HAVE REALLY BEEN! EACH OF THEM IS SURE THAT IT WAS NOT THE VOICE OF HIS OWN COUNTRYMAN. NO WORDS WERE DISTINGUISHABLE TO ANY WITNESS.
"Let us now transport ourselves, in fancy, to the chamber where the murders occurred. What shall we seek here?— The means of egress employed by the murderers."
NO ONE SAW ANYONE ESCAPING DOWN THE STAIRS.
EVERY DOOR WAS LOCKED FROM INSIDE, AND NO ONE SAW ANYONE ESCAPE FROM THE WINDOWS.
THERE IS NO TRAP DOOR, AND THE CHIMNEY IS SO NARROW THAT A CAT CANNOT PASS THROUGH!
"No secret exit could have escaped the vigilance of the police. We are reduced to the windows of the adjoining back room."

"In the room there are two windows. In both their frames, to the right, a very stout nail was found fitted therein, nearly to the head."

"A vigorous attempt to raise the sashes failed. The police were satisfied that egress had not been in these directions."

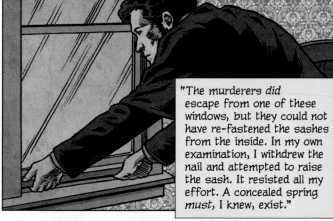

"The murderers *did* escape from one of these windows, but they could not have re-fastened the sashes from the inside. In my own examination, I withdrew the nail and attempted to raise the sash. It resisted all my effort. A concealed spring *must*, I knew, exist."

"I pressed it, and raised the sash. A person passing out through this window might have re-closed it, and the spring would have caught, but the *nail* could not have been replaced."

"A careful search brought to light the hidden spring."

"The conclusion was plain: the assassins must have escaped through the *other* window."

"Supposing the spring upon each sash to be the same, there must be a difference between the *nails*. I discovered and pressed the spring, and then I looked at the nail..."

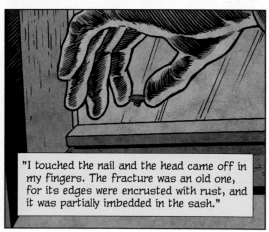

"I touched the nail and the head came off in my fingers. The fracture was an old one, for its edges were encrusted with rust, and it was partially imbedded in the sash."

"I replaced the head portion in the indentation; the fissure was invisible. Pressing the spring, I gently raised the sash for a few inches. The head went up with it."

I CLOSED THE WINDOW, AND THE APPEARANCE OF THE NAIL WAS AGAIN PERFECT. THE ASSASSIN HAD ESCAPED THROUGH THE WINDOW.

DROPPING OF ITS OWN ACCORD AFTER HIS EXIT, IT HAD BECOME FASTENED BY THE SPRING!

"It was the retention of this spring which had been mistaken by the police for that of the nail."

THIS WINDOW IS SECURED. IT CANNOT BE OPENED.

THE NEXT QUESTION IS THAT OF THE MODE OF DESCENT.

UPON THIS POINT I HAD BEEN SATISFIED IN MY WALK WITH YOU AROUND THE BUILDING.

I DID NOT NOTICE ANYTHING!

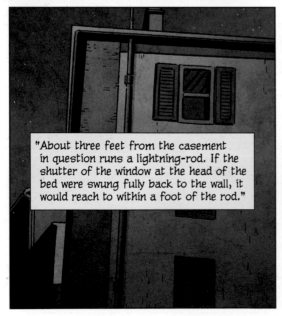

"About three feet from the casement in question runs a lightning-rod. If the shutter of the window at the head of the bed were swung fully back to the wall, it would reach to within a foot of the rod."

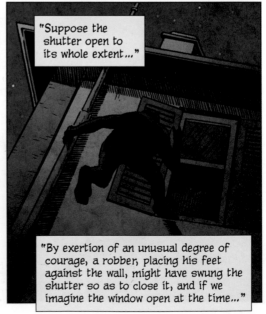

"Suppose the shutter open to its whole extent..."

"By exertion of an unusual degree of courage, a robber, placing his feet against the wall, might have swung the shutter so as to close it, and if we imagine the window open at the time..."

"...he might have swung himself into the room!"

I WOULD SUGGEST THAT BOTH INGRESS AND EGRESS WERE EFFECTED IN THE SAME MANNER. LET US NOW REVERT TO THE INTERIOR OF THE ROOM.

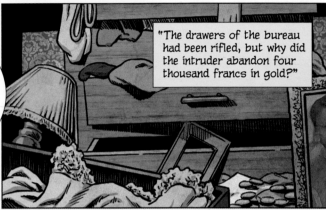

"The drawers of the bureau had been rifled, but why did the intruder abandon four thousand francs in gold?"

KEEPING IN MIND THE POINTS I MENTIONED BEFORE — THAT PECULIAR VOICE AND UNUSUAL AGILITY — LET US GLANCE AT THE BUTCHERY ITSELF!

"Here is a woman strangled to death and thrust up a chimney..."

"Think how great must have been the strength that could have thrust the body up such an aperture so forcibly that several persons together could barely drag it down!"

21

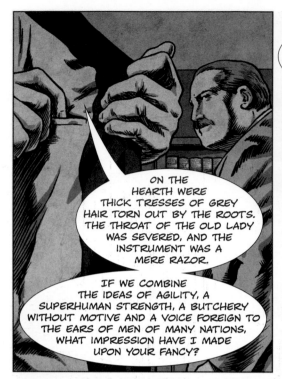

ON THE HEARTH WERE THICK TRESSES OF GREY HAIR TORN OUT BY THE ROOTS. THE THROAT OF THE OLD LADY WAS SEVERED, AND THE INSTRUMENT WAS A MERE RAZOR.

IF WE COMBINE THE IDEAS OF AGILITY, A SUPERHUMAN STRENGTH, A BUTCHERY WITHOUT MOTIVE AND A VOICE FOREIGN TO THE EARS OF MEN OF MANY NATIONS, WHAT IMPRESSION HAVE I MADE UPON YOUR FANCY?

A *MADMAN* HAS DONE THIS DEED — SOME MANIAC ESCAPED FROM A MAISON DE SANITE!

MADMEN ARE OF SOME NATION. HOWEVER INCOHERENT THEIR WORDS, THEY ARE INTELLIGIBLE. BESIDES, THE HAIR OF A MADMAN IS NOT SUCH AS I HOLD IN MY HAND.

I DISENTANGLED THIS TUFT FROM THE FINGERS OF MADAME L. — TELL ME WHAT YOU CAN MAKE OF IT.

THIS HAIR IS MOST UNUSUAL... IT SEEMS NOT HUMAN...

NOW GLANCE AT THIS SKETCH I BASED UPON THE MARKS FOUND ON MADAME'S THROAT. ATTEMPT TO PLACE YOUR FINGERS IN THE RESPECTIVE IMPRESSIONS.

THIS IS THE MARK OF NO *HUMAN* HAND!

READ NOW THIS PASSAGE FROM CUVIER'S SCIENTIFIC STUDY.

It was a descriptive account of the large orangutan of the East Indian Islands...

...The gigantic stature, the strength and activity of those beasts...

At once I understood the full horrors of the murder!

BUT THERE WERE TWO VOICES, AND ONE OF THEM WAS THAT OF A FRENCHMAN.

23

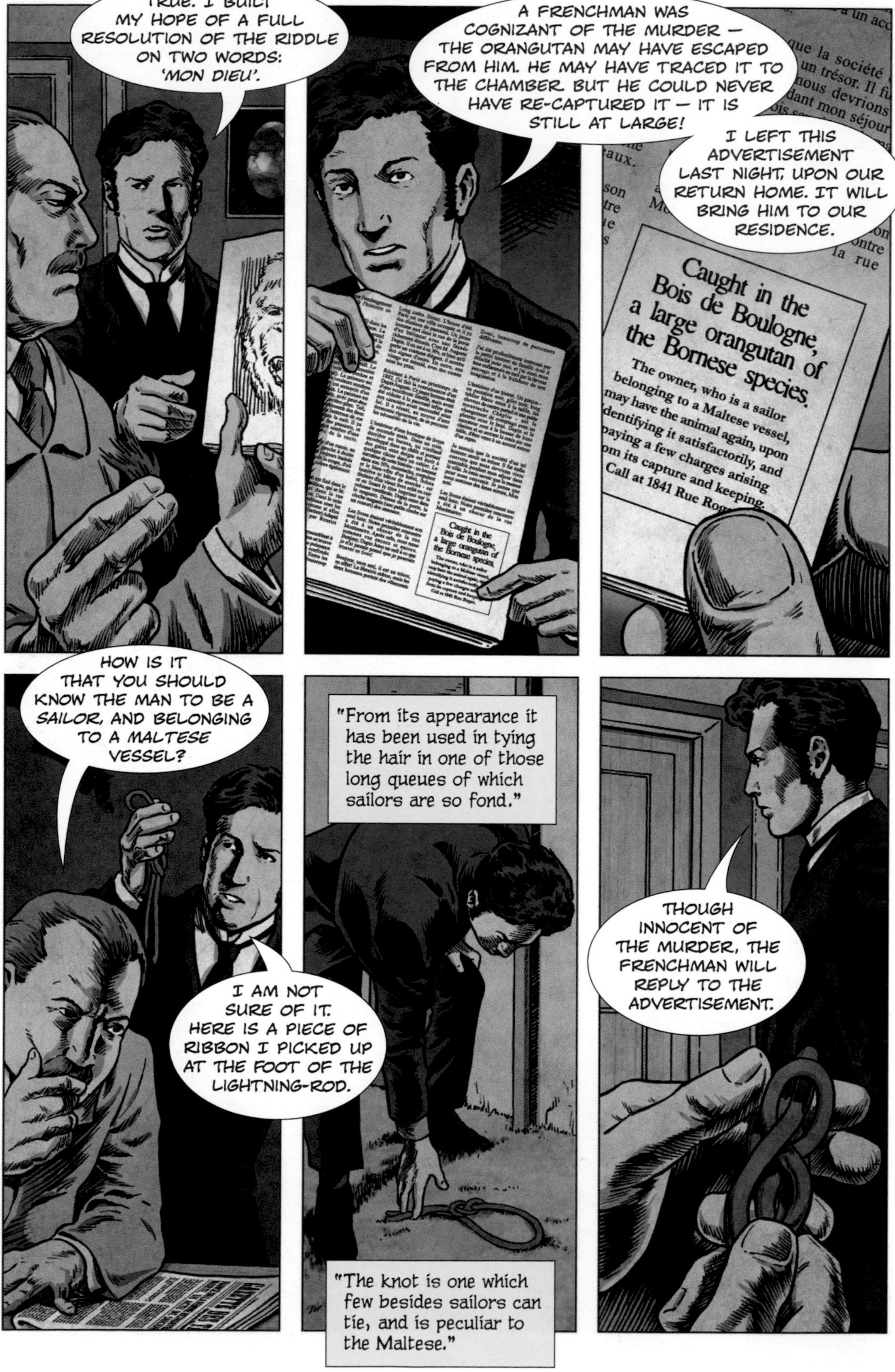
TRUE. I BUILT MY HOPE OF A FULL RESOLUTION OF THE RIDDLE ON TWO WORDS: 'MON DIEU'.
A FRENCHMAN WAS COGNIZANT OF THE MURDER — THE ORANGUTAN MAY HAVE ESCAPED FROM HIM. HE MAY HAVE TRACED IT TO THE CHAMBER BUT HE COULD NEVER HAVE RE-CAPTURED IT — IT IS STILL AT LARGE!
I LEFT THIS ADVERTISEMENT LAST NIGHT, UPON OUR RETURN HOME. IT WILL BRING HIM TO OUR RESIDENCE.
Caught in the Bois de Boulogne, a large orangutan of the Bornese species.
The owner, who is a sailor
belonging to a Maltese vessel,
HOW IS IT THAT YOU SHOULD KNOW THE MAN TO BE A SAILOR, AND BELONGING TO A MALTESE VESSEL?
I AM NOT SURE OF IT. HERE IS A PIECE OF RIBBON I PICKED UP AT THE FOOT OF THE LIGHTNING-ROD.
"From its appearance it has been used in tying the hair in one of those long queues of which sailors are so fond."
"The knot is one which few besides sailors can tie, and is peculiar to the Maltese."
THOUGH INNOCENT OF THE MURDER, THE FRENCHMAN WILL REPLY TO THE ADVERTISEMENT.

HE WILL REASON THUS: "I AM INNOCENT, AND MY ORANGUTAN IS OF GREAT VALUE..."

"...I WILL ANSWER THE ADVERTISEMENT, AND HIDE THE BEAST UNTIL THIS MATTER HAS BLOWN OVER."

We heard a step upon the stair. The visitor seemed to hesitate... Then he stepped up with decision.

THUMP... THUMP-THUMP!

BE READY WITH YOUR PISTOL, BUT NEITHER USE IT NOR SHOW IT UNTIL AT A SIGNAL FROM MYSELF!

COME IN!

KNOCK KNOCK!

GOOD EVENING...

HAVE YOU GOT HIM HERE?

OH NO, HE IS AT A NEARBY STABLE.

SIT DOWN, MY FRIEND! I SUPPOSE YOU HAVE CALLED ABOUT THE ORANGUTAN.

I AM WILLING TO PAY A REWARD FOR THE ANIMAL — ANYTHING IN REASON...

WELL, LET ME THINK... MY REWARD SHALL BE THIS...

...YOU SHALL GIVE ME ALL THE INFORMATION IN YOUR POWER ABOUT THE MURDERS IN THE RUE MORGUE!

I KNOW THAT YOU DID NOT COMMIT THE ACT. BUT AN INNOCENT MAN IS IMPRISONED, CHARGED WITH THE CRIME OF WHICH YOU CAN POINT OUT THE PERPETRATOR.

Dupin then quickly locked the door and placed his pistol upon the table.

SO HELP ME GOD, I AM INNOCENT! I WILL TELL YOU ALL I KNOW ABOUT THIS AFFAIR.

"I made a voyage to the Indian archipelago and landed at Borneo..."

"A companion and I captured the orangutan. My companion afterwards died and the animal fell into my sole possession."

"Later, I succeeded in lodging it at my residence in Paris, where I intended to keep the animal until I could sell it."

"Coming home late one night, I found the beast in my bedroom. Razor in hand, it was attempting the operation of shaving."

"Panicked, the orangutan escaped into the street."

"I followed it, until its attention was arrested by the light from Madame L'Espanaye's window."

"Using the lightning-rod, it clambered up..."

"...grasped the shutter..."

"...and swung itself inside the room."

"I ascended the lightning-rod and leaned over to obtain a glimpse of the interior."

"The sight of blood inflamed the beast into frenzy."

"Then his glance fell upon my face at the window, and his fury became fear."

"I hurried home, dreading the consequences of the butchery, and abandoning the orangutan."

"The orangutan must have escaped from the chamber by the rod."

"It closed the window as it passed through it."

I UNDERSTAND YOUR FEAR, MON AMI. BUT A MAN IS IN PRISON FOR A CRIME HE DID NOT COMMIT.

I CANNOT SLEEP SINCE... I WILL TESTIFY, AND IT WILL BE WHAT IT WILL BE.

The beast was caught by the owner himself, who obtained for it a large sum at the Jardin des Plantes.

Le Bon was released upon our narrative to the police.

EVERYONE SHOULD MIND HIS OWN BUSINESS!

The Prefect of Police could not conceal his discontent.

LET HIM DISCOURSE! I AM SATISFIED WITH HAVING DEFEATED HIM IN HIS OWN CASTLE.

BUT I LIKE HIM FOR THAT BY WHICH HE HAS GAINED HIS REPUTATION — I MEAN THE WAY HE HAS "DE NIER CE QUI EST, ET D'EXPLIQUER CE QUI NE'EST PAS."*

*To deny what is and to explain what is not. — Rousseau

To Violet Vane

a poem by **Edgar Allan Poe**
drawn by **Molly Kiely**

I would not lord it o'er thy heart, **Alas!** I cannot rule my own.

Nor would I rob one loyal thought from him who there should reign alone.

We **both** have found a life-long love; Wherein our weary souls may rest –

Yet may we not, my gentle friend, be each to each the **second best**?

A love which shall be **passion-free!** Fondness as pure as it is sweet –

A bond where all the dearest ties of brother, friend and **cousin** meet.

Such is the union I would frame, that thus we might be **doubly** blest –

With Love to rule our hearts supreme, and friendship to be **second** best.

29

THE FACTS IN THE CASE OF M. VALDEMAR

by
EDGAR
ALLAN
POE

adapted by
TOM POMPLUN
illustrated by
MICHAEL MANNING

The extraordinary case of M. Valdemar has recently become the source of a number of unpleasant misrepresentations, and it is now necessary that I give the facts as I comprehend them.

My attention, for the last three years, had been repeatedly drawn to the subject of mesmerism...

...and it occurred to me that in the series of experiments made hitherto, there had been a very remarkable omission —

No person had as yet been mesmerized in *articulo mortis*.

It remained to be seen, first, if in such condition there existed in the patient any susceptibility to magnetic influence; secondly, whether the influence was affected by the condition; thirdly, to what extent the encroachment of death might be arrested by the process.

In looking for a test subject, I thought of my friend, the well-known author M. Ernest Valdemar.

His temperament rendered him a good subject for mesmeric experiment. On several occasions I had put him to sleep with little difficulty, but was disappointed with the results.

His will was at no period thoroughly under my control, and in regard to clairvoyance, I could accomplish with him nothing reliable.

I always attributed my failure to the poor state of his health.

For some months previous to my becoming acquainted with him, his physicians had declared him a victim of tuberculosis. It was M. Valdemar's custom to discuss calmly his approaching dissolution as of a matter neither to be avoided nor regretted.

I thus spoke to him frankly of my proposed experiment; and to my surprise, his interest seemed vividly excited.

His disease was of that character which would admit of exact calculation in respect to the date of its termination; and it was arranged between us that he would send for me twenty-four hours before his expected decease.

My Dear Pierce,
You may as well come now. The doctors are agreed that I cannot hold out beyond tomorrow midnight; and I think they have hit the time very nearly.
Valdemar.

I received this note within half an hour after it was written, and in fifteen minutes more I was in the dying man's chamber. I had not seen him for ten days, and was appalled by the fearful alteration which the brief interval had wrought in him.

His face wore a leaden hue; his eyes were lustreless; and his emaciation was extreme.

He retained, nevertheless, his mental power and spoke with distinctness. Doctors Dierdrich and Farrell were in attendance.

I took these gentlemen aside, and obtained from them an account of the patient's condition. The opinion of both physicians was that M. Valdemar would die about midnight on the morrow. It was then seven o'clock on Saturday evening.

The doctors had bidden Valdemar a final farewell, and it had not been their intention to return...

But at my request they agreed to look in upon the patient about ten the next night.

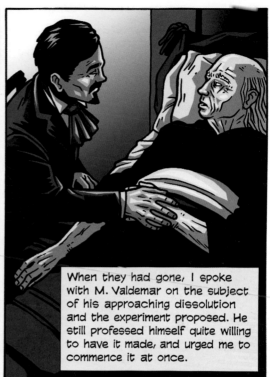

When they had gone, I spoke with M. Valdemar on the subject of his approaching dissolution and the experiment proposed. He still professed himself quite willing to have it made, and urged me to commence it at once.

I did not feel myself at liberty to engage in a task of this character with only the nurse as witness.

I therefore postponed the operations until eight the next night, when I was expecting Mr. Theodore Lloyd, a medical student of my acquaintance.

Mr. Lloyd was so kind as to accede to my desire that he would take notes of all that occurred.

It is from his memoranda that what I now have to relate is, for the most part, drawn.

It had been my design, originally, to wait for the physicians; but I was induced to proceed, first, by the urgent entreaties of M. Valdemar, and secondly, by my conviction that I had not a moment to lose, as he was evidently sinking fast.

It wanted about five minutes of eight when I asked the patient to state, as distinctly as he could, to Mr. Lloyd, whether he was entirely willing that I should proceed with the experiment.

YES, I WISH TO BE MESMERIZED – I FEAR YOU HAVE DEFERRED IT TOO LONG.

I immediately commenced the passes. He was clearly influenced with the first lateral stroke of my hand across his forehead...

But though I exerted all my powers for some time, no further perceptible effect was induced.

At ten o'clock Doctors Dierdrich and Ferrell called, by appointment.

I explained to them what I designed, and they opposed no objection, since the patient was already in the death agony.

I resumed the procedure. By this time the patient's breathing was shallow, and his pulse imperceptible.

This condition was nearly unaltered for a quarter of an hour. At the expiration of this period, a deep sigh escaped from the bosom of the dying man, and the breathing became minimal. The patient's extremities were of an icy coldness.

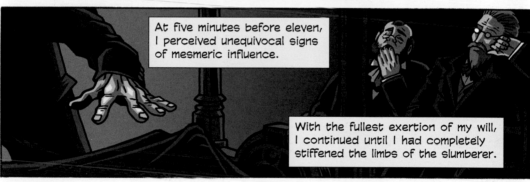

At five minutes before eleven, I perceived unequivocal signs of mesmeric influence.

With the fullest exertion of my will, I continued until I had completely stiffened the limbs of the slumberer.

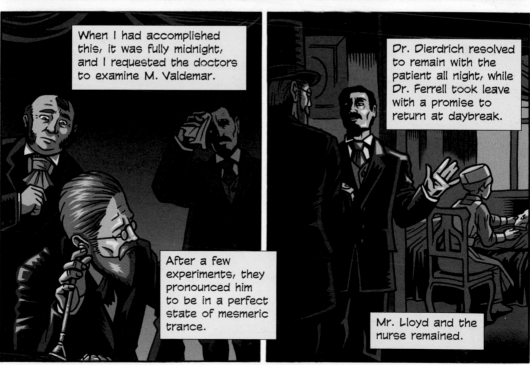

When I had accomplished this, it was fully midnight, and I requested the doctors to examine M. Valdemar.

After a few experiments, they pronounced him to be in a perfect state of mesmeric trance.

Dr. Dierdrich resolved to remain with the patient all night, while Dr. Ferrell took leave with a promise to return at daybreak.

Mr. Lloyd and the nurse remained.

We left M. Valdemar undisturbed until about three a.m., when I found him in precisely the same condition: the pulse was imperceptible; the breathing scarcely noticeable; and the limbs were as rigid and as cold as marble. Still, the general appearance was not that of death.

As an experiment, I attempted to influence his right arm into pursuit of my own.

His arm feebly followed every direction I assigned it. I determined to hazard a brief conversation.

M. VALDEMAR, ARE YOU ASLEEP?

He made no answer, but I perceived a tremor about the lips, and was thus induced to repeat the question.

M. VALDEMAR ...

ARE YOU ASLEEP?

YES — ASLEEP NOW. DO NOT WAKE ME! LET ME DIE SO!

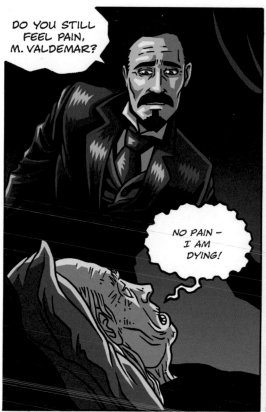

DO YOU STILL FEEL PAIN, M. VALDEMAR?

NO PAIN — I AM DYING!

I did not think it advisable to disturb him further just then...

Nothing more was said or done until the arrival of Dr. Ferrell in the morning.

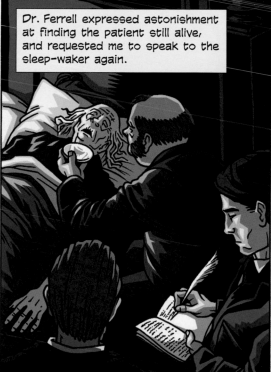

Dr. Ferrell expressed astonishment at finding the patient still alive, and requested me to speak to the sleep-waker again.

M. VALDEMAR, DO YOU STILL SLEEP?

As before, some minutes elapsed ere a reply was made. At my fourth repetition of the question, he spoke very faintly.

YES; STILL ASLEEP... DYING.

37

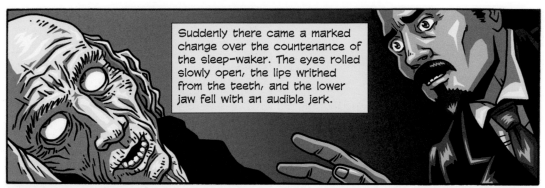

Suddenly there came a marked change over the countenance of the sleep-waker. The eyes rolled slowly open, the lips writhed from the teeth, and the lower jaw fell with an audible jerk.

There was no longer the faintest sign of vitality in M. Valdemar. Concluding him to be dead, the doctors were consigning him to the charge of the nurse, when a vibratory motion was observed in the tongue.

There then issued from the motionless jaws a voice such as it would be madness in me to attempt describing.

It seemed to reach from a vast distance, as from some deep cavern within the earth!

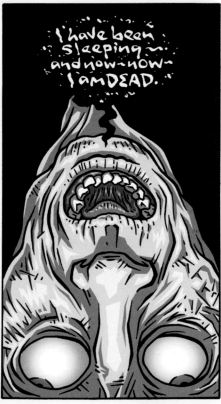

I have been sleeping ~ and now ~ now ~ I am DEAD.

No person present even affected to deny the horror these words conveyed.

Mr. Lloyd swooned. The nurse fled the chamber, and could not be induced to return.

My own impressions I would not pretend to render intelligible to the reader.

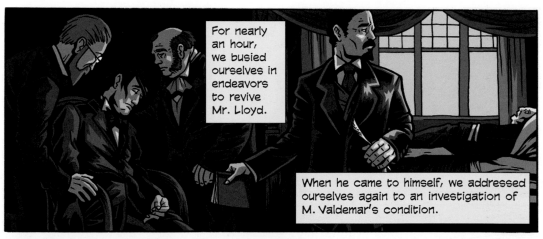

For nearly an hour, we busied ourselves in endeavors to revive Mr. Lloyd.

When he came to himself, we addressed ourselves again to an investigation of M. Valdemar's condition.

There was no evidence of respiration.

An attempt to draw blood from the arm failed.

I addressed M. Valdemar a question...

He seemed to be making an effort to reply, but had no longer sufficient volition.

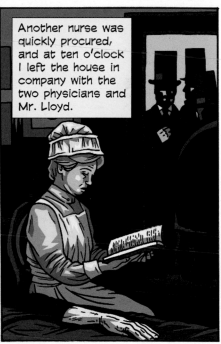

Another nurse was quickly procured, and at ten o'clock I left the house in company with the two physicians and Mr. Lloyd.

From that day until the close of last week — an interval of nearly seven months — we continued to make daily calls at M. Valdemar's house. All this time the sleep-waker remained exactly as I have last described him.

It was on Friday last that we finally resolved to make the attempt to awaken him...

...and it is the unfortunate result of this experiment which has given rise to so much of what I cannot help thinking unwarranted popular feeling.

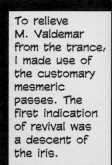
To relieve M. Valdemar from the trance, I made use of the customary mesmeric passes. The first indication of revival was a descent of the iris.

This lowering of the pupils was accompanied by the profuse outflowing of a yellowish ichor of a highly offensive odor.

Dr. Farrell then intimated a desire to have me put a question to the patient.

M. VALDEMAR, CAN YOU EXPLAIN TO US WHAT ARE YOUR WISHES NOW?

There was an instant response: the same hideous voice which I have already described broke forth.

FOR God's sake! ~ put me To sleep ~ or, quick! ~wakenme~ I say to you that I am dead!

I made an endeavor to calm the patient; but, failing in this, I attempted to awaken him.

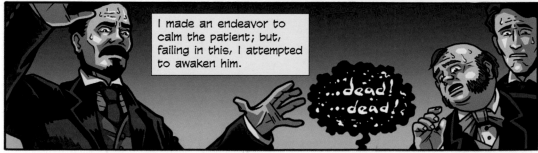
...dead! ...dead!

For what occurred next, however, it is quite impossible that *any* human being could have been prepared...

As I rapidly made the mesmeric passes, the sufferer's whole frame — within the space of a single minute — absolutely rotted away beneath my hands!

Upon the bed, before the whole company, there lay a nearly liquid mass of loathsome, detestable putrescence!

A DREAM WITHIN A DREAM

by Edgar Allan Poe.

ART * N. BLANDEN *

TAKE THIS KISS UPON THE BROW! AND, IN PARTING FROM YOU NOW,

THUS MUCH LET ME AVOW— YOU ARE NOT WRONG, WHO DEEM THAT MY DAYS HAVE BEEN A DREAM:

YET IF HOPE HAS FLOWN AWAY IN A NIGHT, OR IN A DAY,

IN A VISION, OR IN NONE IS IT THEREFORE THE LESS GONE?

ALL THAT WE SEE OR SEEM IS BUT A DREAM WITHIN A DREAM.

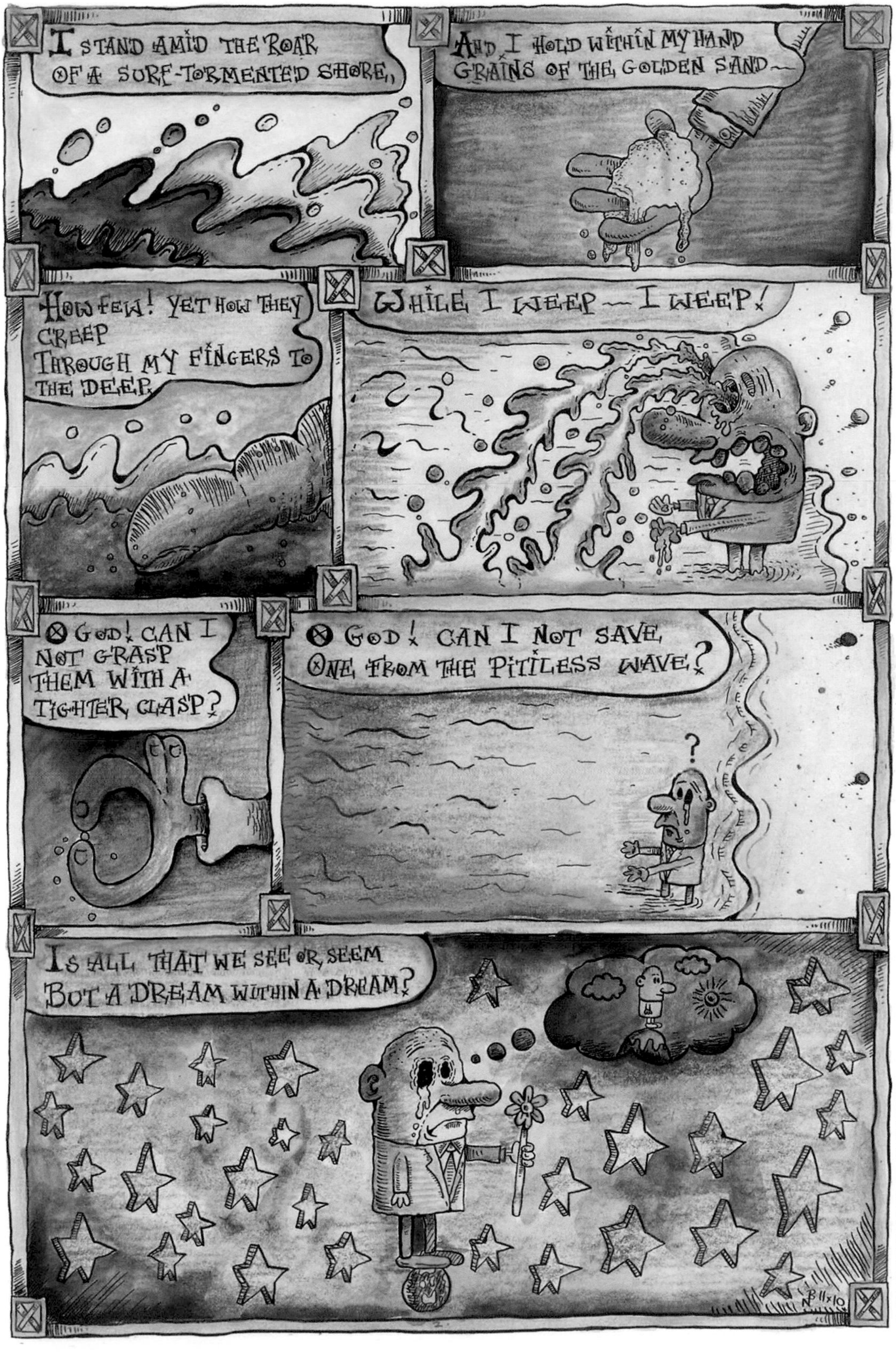
I STAND AMID THE ROAR
OF A SURF-TORMENTED SHORE,
AND I HOLD WITHIN MY HAND
GRAINS OF THE GOLDEN SAND—
HOW FEW! YET HOW THEY CREEP
THROUGH MY FINGERS TO THE DEEP,
WHILE I WEEP—I WEEP!
O GOD! CAN I NOT GRASP THEM WITH A TIGHTER CLASP?
O GOD! CAN I NOT SAVE
ONE FROM THE PITILESS WAVE?
IS ALL THAT WE SEE OR SEEM
BUT A DREAM WITHIN A DREAM?

Dicebant mihi sodales, si sepulchrum amicae visitarem, curas meas aliquantulum forelevatas. — Ebn Zaiat

Berenice

by Edgar Allan Poe
adapted by **Tom Pomplun**
illustrated by
Nelson Evergreen

Misery is manifold. The wretchedness of earth is multiform. How is it that from beauty I have derived a type of unloveliness? But as evil is a consequence of good, so, in fact, out of joy is sorrow born.

My name is Egaeus; that of my family I will not mention. Yet there are no towers in the land more time-honored than my gloomy, gray, hereditary home.

In these halls I loitered away my boyhood in books, and dissipated my youth in reverie.

As the years rolled away, and the noon of manhood found me still in the mansion of my fathers, the realities of the world affected me as visions, while the land of dreams became not just the material of my everyday existence...

...but indeed that existence in itself.

Berenice and I were cousins, and we grew up together in my paternal halls. Yet differently we grew—I, ill of health, and buried in gloom—she, agile, graceful, and overflowing with energy.

Berenice! Ah, vividly is her image before me now, as in the early days of her light-heartedness and joy!

And then disease—a fatal disease—fell upon her frame; and the spirit of change swept over her, pervading her mind, her habits, and her character.

Alas, the destroyer came and went! And the victim—I knew her not—or knew her no longer as Berenice.

Among the maladies suffered by my cousin was a species of epilepsy not unfrequently terminating in trance—a trance very nearly resembling dissolution...

...and from which her recovery was, in most instances, startlingly abrupt.

In the meantime my own disease grew rapidly upon me. This monomania, if I must so term it, consisted in a morbid irritability of those properties of the mind termed the attentive.

To muse for hours, with my attention riveted to some frivolous device on the margin of a book; to lose myself, for an entire night, in watching the embers of a fire; to dream away whole days over the perfume of a flower...

...to lose all sense of motion or physical existence...

...such were a few of the vagaries induced by a condition of the mental faculties bidding defiance to analysis or explanation.

My books, if they did not actually serve to irritate the disorder, partook, in their imaginative and inconsequential nature, of the characteristic qualities of the disorder itself.

Mortus est Dei filius; credible est quia ineptum est: et sepultus resurrexit; certum est quia impossibile est

I well remember Tertullian's paradoxical sentence, "That the Son of God died is wholly credible because it is unsound; and that, buried, he rose again, is certain because it is impossible," which occupied many weeks of fruitless investigation.

46

Thus, shaken from its balance only by trivial things, my reason bore resemblance to that ocean-crag spoken of by Ptolemy, which steadily resisting the attacks of human violence, and the fiercer fury of the waters and the winds, trembled only to the touch of a flower.

And although it might appear that the alteration in the moral condition of Berenice would afford exercise of that intense meditation whose nature I have been at some trouble in explaining, yet such was not the case.

In the lucid intervals of my infirmity, her calamity, indeed, gave me pain. But true to its own character, my disorder reveled in the less important but more startling changes wrought in the physical frame of Berenice.

During the brightest days of her beauty, I had never loved her.

In the strange anomaly of my existence, I had seen her, not as the living and breathing Berenice, but as a dream; not as a thing to admire, but to analyze.

And, in an evil moment, I spoke to her of marriage.

At length the period of our nuptials was approaching when, upon an afternoon in the winter of the year, I sat alone in the library...

...and, uplifting my eyes, I saw that Berenice stood before me.

She spoke no word; and an icy chill ran through my frame.

Her emaciation was excessive, and not one vestige of her former being lurked in any line of contour. My burning glance at length fell upon the face.

The eyes were lifeless and lustreless, and I shrank involuntarily from their glassy stare to the contemplation of the thin and shrunken lips.

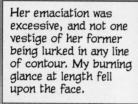

They parted; and in a smile of peculiar meaning...

...the teeth of Berenice disclosed themselves slowly to my view.

Would to God that I had never beheld them, or that, having done so, I had died!

The shutting of a door disturbed me, and I found that my cousin had departed from the chamber. But from the disordered chamber of my brain, had not departed, and would not be driven away, the white and ghastly spectrum of the teeth.

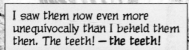

I saw them now even more unequivocally than I beheld them then. The teeth! — the teeth!

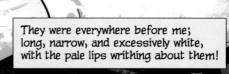

They were everywhere before me; long, narrow, and excessively white, with the pale lips writhing about them!

Then came the full fury of my monomania, and I struggled in vain against its irresistible influence. I had no thoughts but for the teeth. For these I longed with a frenzied desire. All other matters became absorbed in their single contemplation.

They — they alone — became the essence of my mental life. I held them in every light. I turned them in every attitude. I dwelt upon their peculiarities. I pondered upon their conformation.

I coveted them madly! I felt that their possession alone could ever restore me to peace — could give me back to reason.

And the evening closed in upon me thus — and the day again dawned — and the mists of a second night were gathering — and still I sat in that solitary room — and still the phantasma of the teeth maintained its terrible ascendancy.

At length there broke in upon my dreams a cry as of horror and dismay; and then succeeded the sound of troubled voices, intermingled with low moanings of sorrow.

I arose from my seat, and throwing open the door, saw standing out in the ante-chamber a servant, all in tears, who told me that Berenice was — no more!

She had been seized with epilepsy in the early morning, and now, at the closing in of the night, the crypt was ready for its tenant, and all the preparations for the burial were completed.

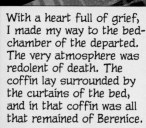

With a heart full of grief, I made my way to the bedchamber of the departed. The very atmosphere was redolent of death. The coffin lay surrounded by the curtains of the bed, and in that coffin was all that remained of Berenice.

The peculiar smell of the coffin sickened me; and I fancied a deleterious odor was already exhaling from the body. I would have given worlds to escape — to fly from the pernicious influence of mortality.

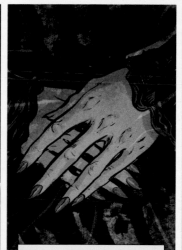

Then — God of heaven! — was it possible? Or was it indeed the finger of the enshrouded dead that stirred? Frozen with awe I slowly raised my eyes to the countenance of the corpse.

The livid lips were wreathed into a smile, and, through the enveloping gloom, once again there glared upon me the white, and glistening, and ghastly teeth of Berenice!

I fled from the room in mortal terror, and retreated to my own chambers.

Late that night:

And now, I find myself sitting alone in the library. It seems I have awakened from a confusing dream. I know that it is midnight, and I am aware, that since the setting of the sun, Berenice has been interred.

But of that dreary period which intervened I have no definite comprehension. Yet its memory is replete with horror — horror more horrible from being vague, and terror more terrible from ambiguity.

I strive to remember, but in vain; while ever and anon, like the spirit of a departed sound, a shrill and piercing shriek seems to be ringing in my ears.

I have done a deed — what was it?

WHAT WAS IT?

On my desk lay a little box. It was of no remarkable character, and I had seen it frequently before; but how came it there, upon my table, and why did I shudder in regarding it?

My eyes dropped to the open pages of a book, and to a sentence underscored therein. The words were the singular but simple ones of the poet Ebn Zaiat:

"My companions told me I might find some little alleviation of my misery, in visiting the grave of my beloved."

Dicebant mihi sodales si sepulcrum amicae visitarem, curas meas aliquantulum fore levatas.

Why, as I perused these words, did the hairs of my head erect themselves on end, and the blood of my body become congealed within my veins?

There came a tap at the library door, and a pale menial entered.

His looks were wild with terror as he told of a strange cry disturbing the silence of the night...

...of a violated grave...

...of a disfigured body, enshrouded, yet still breathing — still alive!

He pointed to my garments; they were bloody and clotted with gore.

He directed my attention to some object on the floor.

I looked at it without recognition.

With a shriek, I grasped for the box that lay upon the desk.

In my tremor, it slipped from my hands, fell heavily, and burst open...

...and from it, with a rattling sound, there rolled out thirty-two small, white objects that were scattered across the floor!

WORDS BY **EDGAR ALLAN POE**   PICTURES BY ROGER LANGRIDGE

AND, AS HIS STRENGTH FAILED HIM AT LENGTH, HE MET A PILGRIM SHADOW.

"SHADOW," SAID HE, "WHERE CAN IT BE ~ THIS LAND OF ELDORADO?"

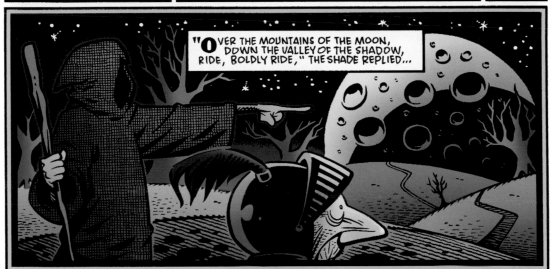

"OVER THE MOUNTAINS OF THE MOON, DOWN THE VALLEY OF THE SHADOW, RIDE, BOLDLY RIDE," THE SHADE REPLIED...

"... IF YOU SEEK FOR ELDORADO."

HOP-FROG

adapted by Rod Lott

illustrated by Lisa K. Weber

I NEVER KNEW ANYONE SO KEENLY ALIVE TO A JOKE AS THE KING.

TO TELL A JOKE WELL WAS THE SUREST ROAD TO HIS FAVOR.

HIS SEVEN MINISTERS WERE ALL JOKERS. THEY ALL TOOK AFTER THE KING IN BEING CORPULENT, OILY MEN. WHETHER PEOPLE GROW FAT BY JOKING, I HAVE NEVER BEEN ABLE TO DETERMINE.

JESTERS HAD NOT GONE OUT OF FASHION AT COURT. SEVERAL GREAT CONTINENTAL "POWERS" STILL RETAINED THEIR "FOOLS," EXPECTED TO BE READY WITH SHARP WITTICISMS AT A MOMENT'S NOTICE.

OUR KING'S FOOL WAS NOT ONLY A FOOL. HIS VALUE WAS TREBLED BY BEING ALSO A DWARF AND A CRIPPLE.

IN 99 CASES OUT OF 100, JESTERS ARE FAT, ROUND AND UNWIELDY, SO IT WAS NO SMALL SOURCE OF SELF-GRATULATION WITH OUR KING THAT IN HOP-FROG, HE POSSESSED A TRIPLICATE TREASURE.

I BELIEVE THE NAME "HOP-FROG" WAS NOT GIVEN TO HIM AT BAPTISM, BUT CONFERRED UPON HIM BY GENERAL CONSENT OF THE MINISTERS ON ACCOUNT OF HIS INABILITY TO WALK AS OTHERS.

HOP-FROG COULD ONLY GET ALONG BY A SORT OF INTERJECTIONAL GAIT – SOMETHING BETWEEN A LEAP AND A WRIGGLE.

A MOVEMENT THAT AFFORDED ILLIMITABLE AMUSEMENT.

ALTHOUGH HOP-FROG COULD WALK ONLY WITH GREAT PAIN, THE MUSCULAR POWER NATURE SEEMED TO BESTOW UPON HIS ARMS, BY WAY OF COMPENSATION, ENABLED HIM TO PERFORM MANY FEATS OF DEXTERITY.

AT SUCH CLIMBING EXERCISES, HE CERTAINLY MUCH MORE RESEMBLED A SQUIRREL, OR A MONKEY, THAN A FROG.

FROM SOME BARBAROUS REGION, HOP-FROG AND A YOUNG GIRL LITTLE LESS DWARFISH, HAD BEEN FORCIBLY CARRIED OFF FROM THEIR HOMES AND SENT AS PRESENTS TO THE KING.

HOP-FROG AND TRIPPETTA SOON BECAME SWORN FRIENDS.

HE WAS BY NO MEANS POPULAR, BUT THE MARVELOUS DANCER, ON ACCOUNT OF HER BEAUTY, WAS UNIVERSALLY ADMIRED.

SHE USED HER INFLUENCE, WHENEVER SHE COULD, FOR HIS BENEFIT.

ON SOME GRAND OCCASION - I FORGOT WHAT - THE KING DETERMINED TO HAVE A MASQUERADE, SO THE TALENTS OF HOP-FROG AND TRIPPETTA WERE SURE TO BE CALLED INTO PLAY.

HOP-FROG WAS INVENTIVE IN GETTING UP PAGEANTS, SUGGESTING CHARACTERS AND ARRANGING COSTUMES.

THE NIGHT FOR THE FÊTE HAD ARRIVED. A GORGEOUS HALL HAD BEEN FITTED UP, UNDER TRIPPETTA'S EYE.

AS FOR COSTUMES, THE KING AND HIS SEVEN MINISTERS HESITATED, PROBABLY ON ACCOUNT OF BEING SO FAT. AS A LAST RESORT, THEY SENT FOR TRIPPETTA AND HOP-FROG.

..BUT THE KING LOVED HIS PRACTICAL JOKES.

THEY FOUND THE KING SITTING AT HIS WINE.

COME HERE, HOP-FROG! BE MERRY!

SWALLOW THIS BUMPER TO THE HEALTH OF YOUR ABSENT FRIENDS!

HE KNEW HOP-FROG WAS NOT FOND OF WINE, FOR IT EXCITED THE POOR CRIPPLE ALMOST TO MADNESS, AND MADNESS IS NO COMFORTABLE FEELING...

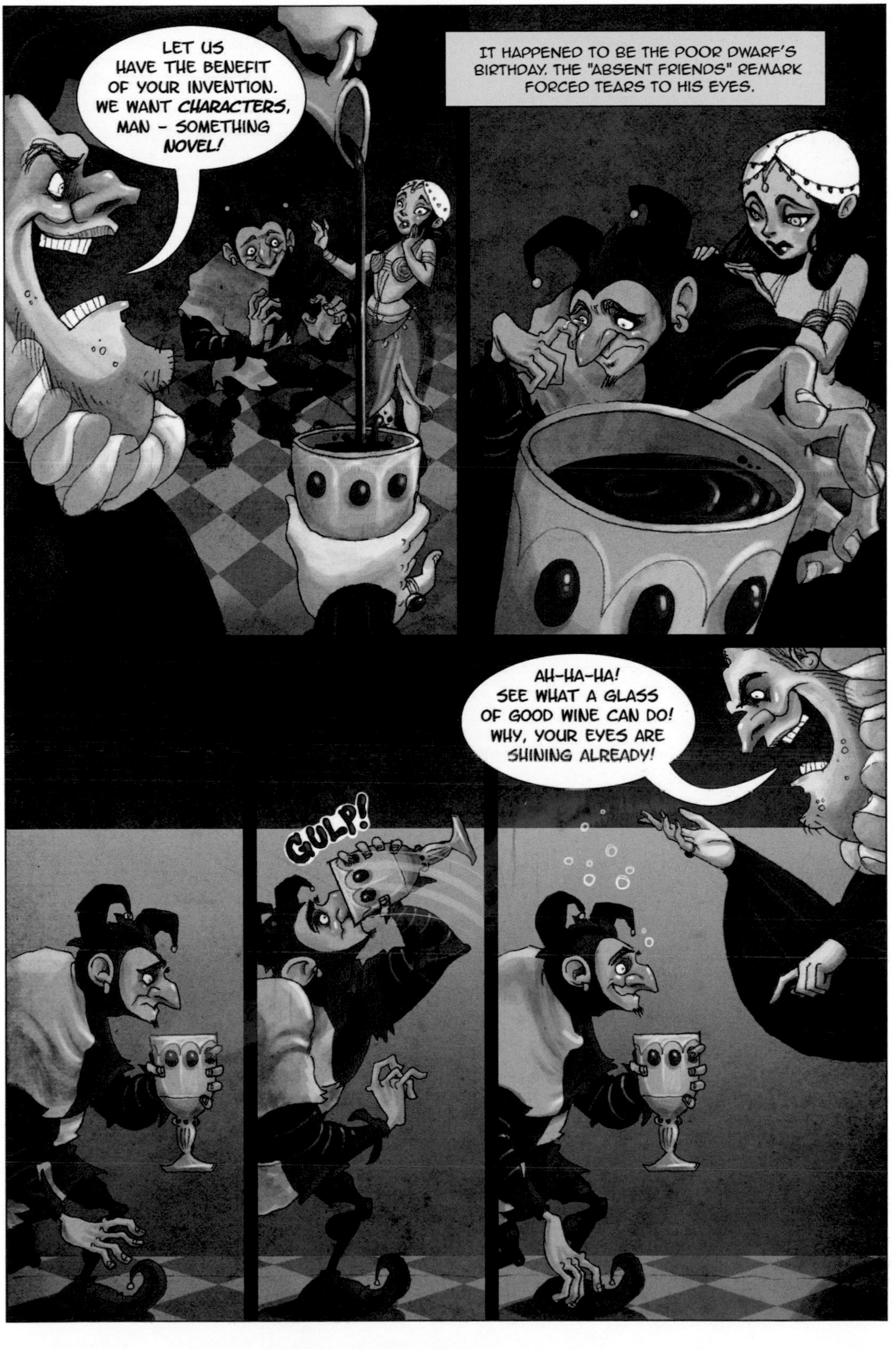
LET US HAVE THE BENEFIT OF YOUR INVENTION. WE WANT CHARACTERS, MAN - SOMETHING NOVEL!
IT HAPPENED TO BE THE POOR DWARF'S BIRTHDAY. THE "ABSENT FRIENDS" REMARK FORCED TEARS TO HIS EYES.
GULP!
AH-HA-HA! SEE WHAT A GLASS OF GOOD WINE CAN DO! WHY, YOUR EYES ARE SHINING ALREADY!

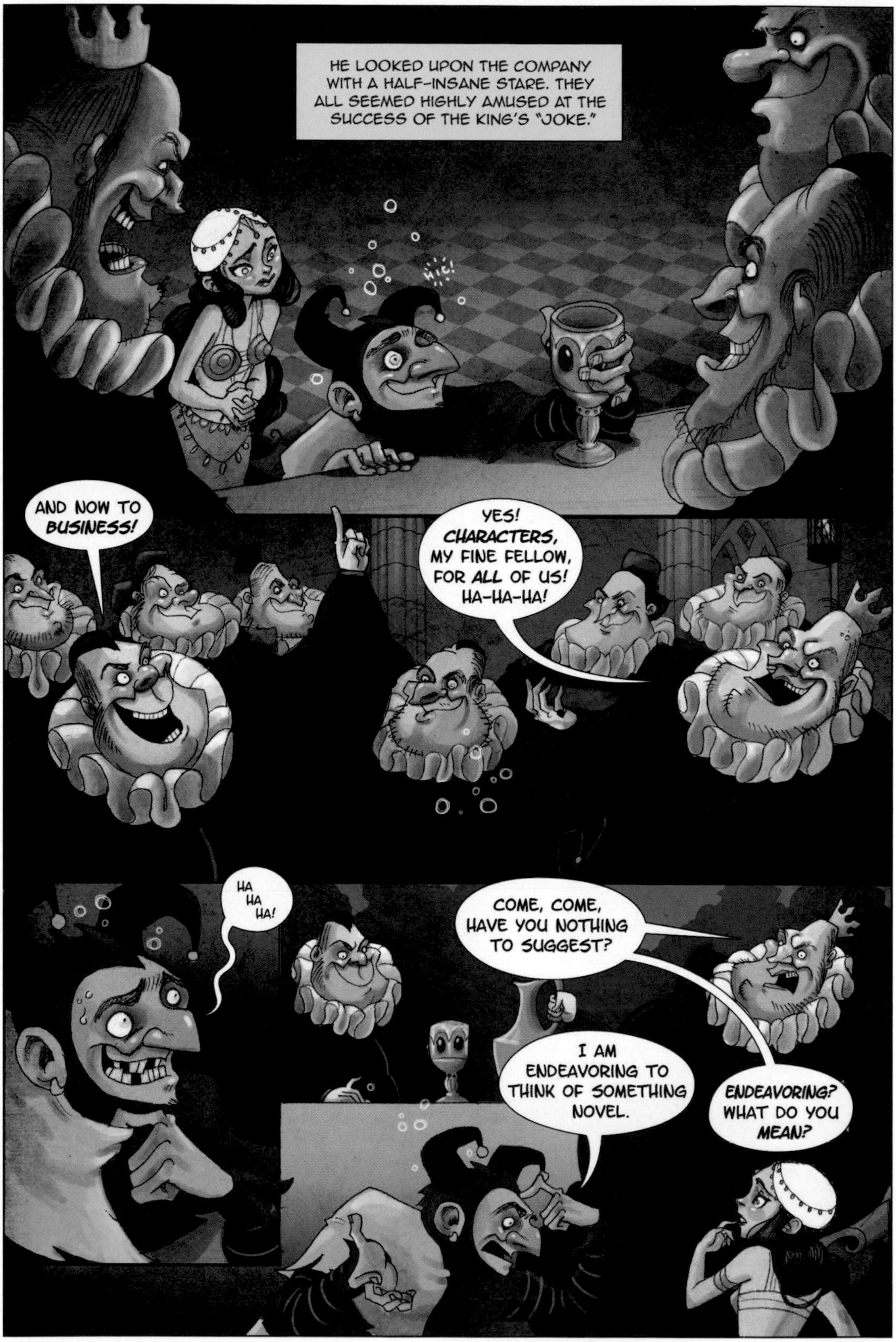
HE LOOKED UPON THE COMPANY WITH A HALF-INSANE STARE. THEY ALL SEEMED HIGHLY AMUSED AT THE SUCCESS OF THE KING'S "JOKE."
HIC!
AND NOW TO BUSINESS!
YES! CHARACTERS, MY FINE FELLOW, FOR ALL OF US! HA-HA-HA!
HA HA HA!
COME, COME, HAVE YOU NOTHING TO SUGGEST?
I AM ENDEAVORING TO THINK OF SOMETHING NOVEL.
ENDEAVORING? WHAT DO YOU MEAN?

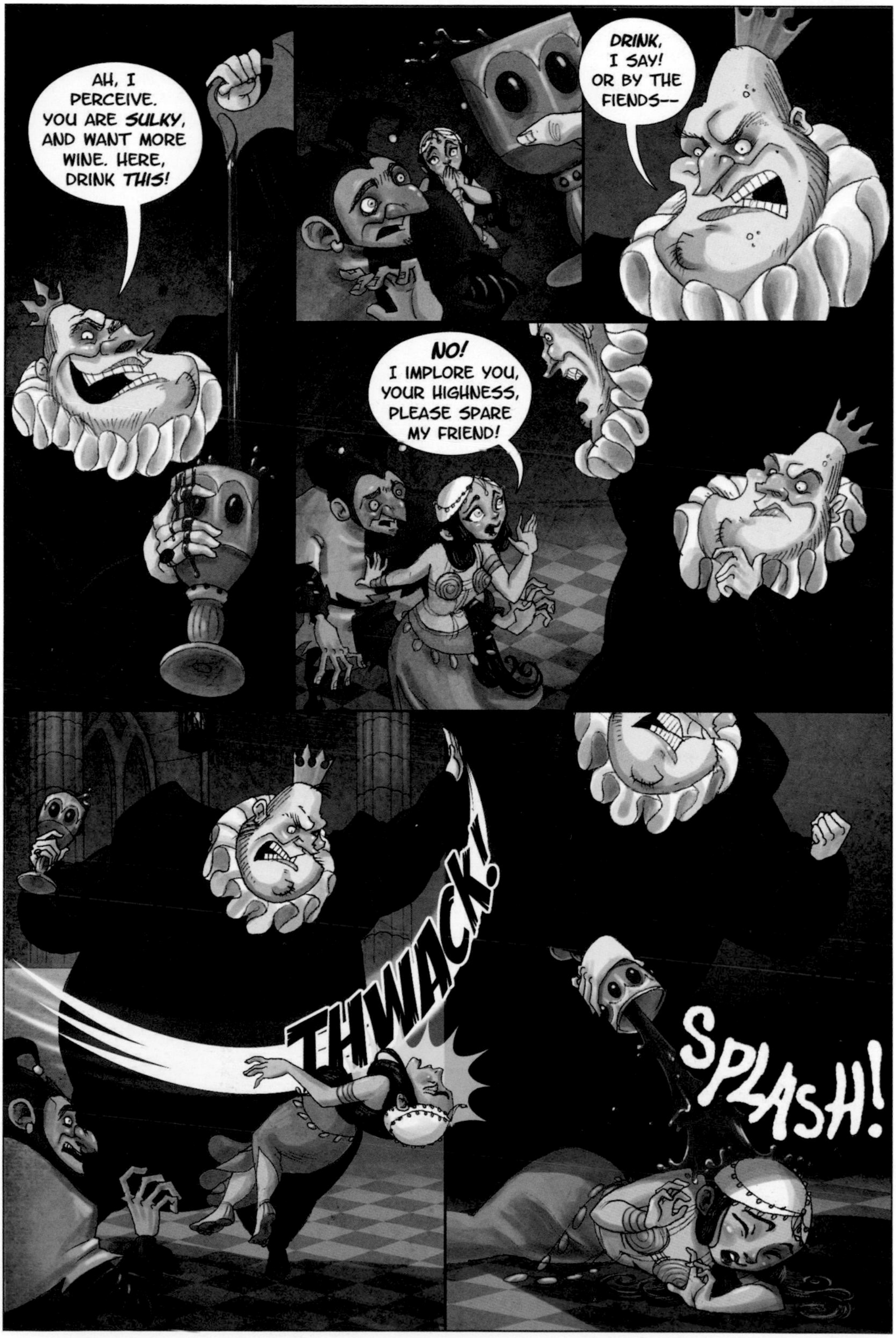
AH, I PERCEIVE. YOU ARE SULKY, AND WANT MORE WINE. HERE, DRINK THIS!
DRINK, I SAY! OR BY THE FIENDS--
NO! I IMPLORE YOU, YOUR HIGHNESS, PLEASE SPARE MY FRIEND!
THWACK!
SPLASH!

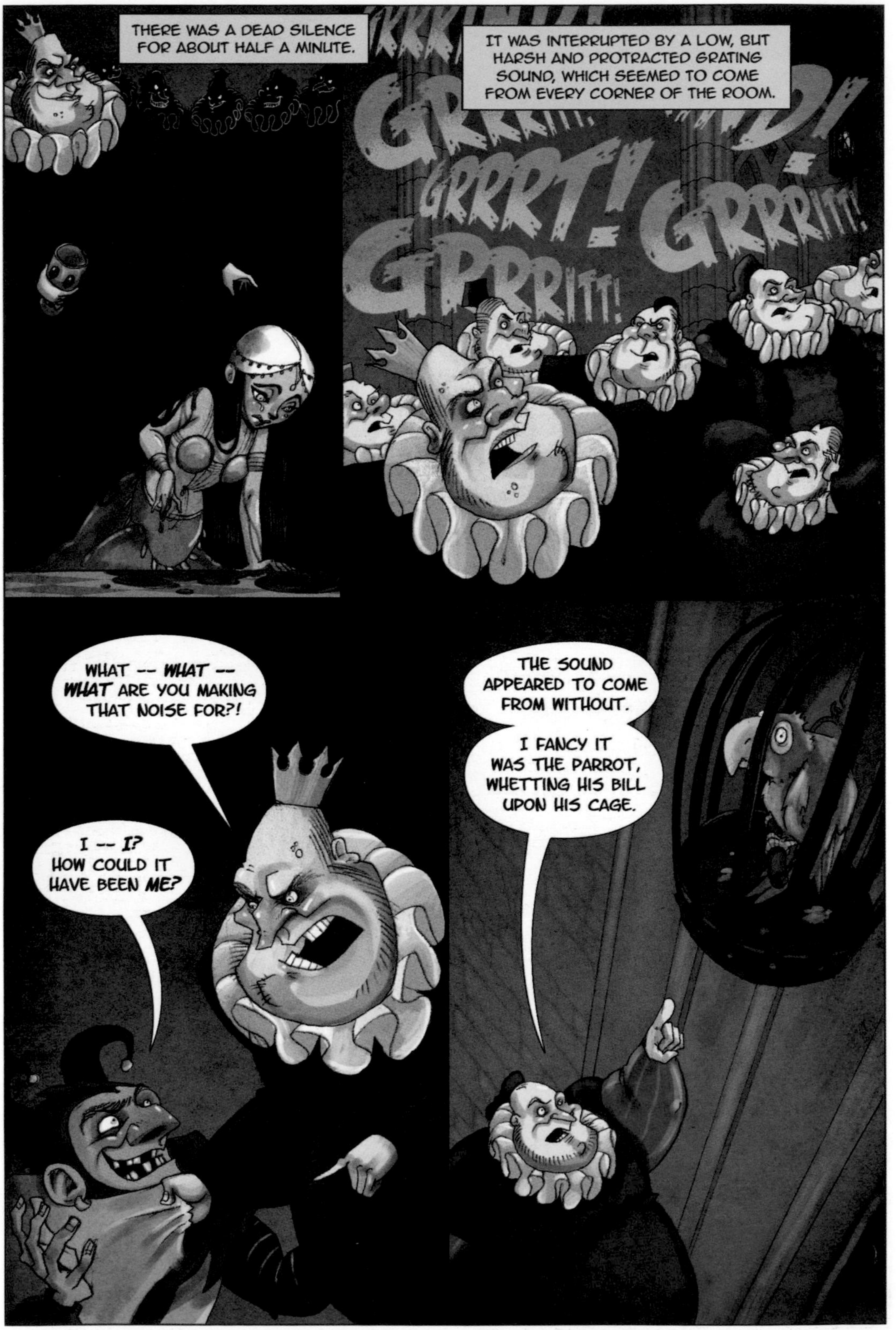
THERE WAS A DEAD SILENCE FOR ABOUT HALF A MINUTE.
IT WAS INTERRUPTED BY A LOW, BUT HARSH AND PROTRACTED GRATING SOUND, WHICH SEEMED TO COME FROM EVERY CORNER OF THE ROOM.
GRRRT! GRRRIT! GRRRITT!
WHAT -- WHAT -- WHAT ARE YOU MAKING THAT NOISE FOR?!
I -- I? HOW COULD IT HAVE BEEN ME?
THE SOUND APPEARED TO COME FROM WITHOUT.
I FANCY IT WAS THE PARROT, WHETTING HIS BILL UPON HIS CAGE.

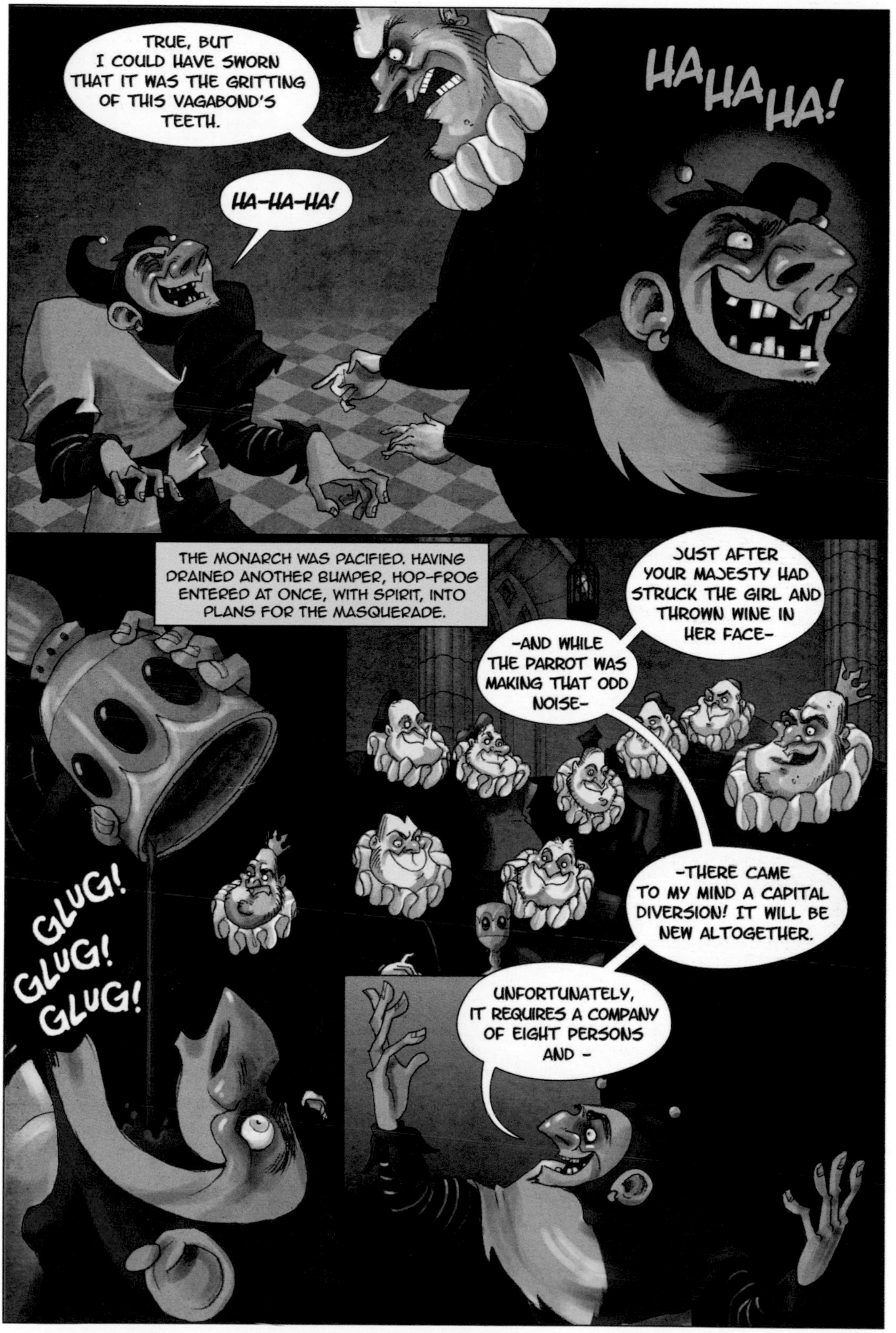
TRUE, BUT I COULD HAVE SWORN THAT IT WAS THE GRITTING OF THIS VAGABOND'S TEETH.
HA-HA-HA!
HA HA HA!
THE MONARCH WAS PACIFIED. HAVING DRAINED ANOTHER BUMPER, HOP-FROG ENTERED AT ONCE, WITH SPIRIT, INTO PLANS FOR THE MASQUERADE.
GLUG! GLUG! GLUG!
JUST AFTER YOUR MAJESTY HAD STRUCK THE GIRL AND THROWN WINE IN HER FACE-
-AND WHILE THE PARROT WAS MAKING THAT ODD NOISE-
-THERE CAME TO MY MIND A CAPITAL DIVERSION! IT WILL BE NEW ALTOGETHER.
UNFORTUNATELY, IT REQUIRES A COMPANY OF EIGHT PERSONS AND -

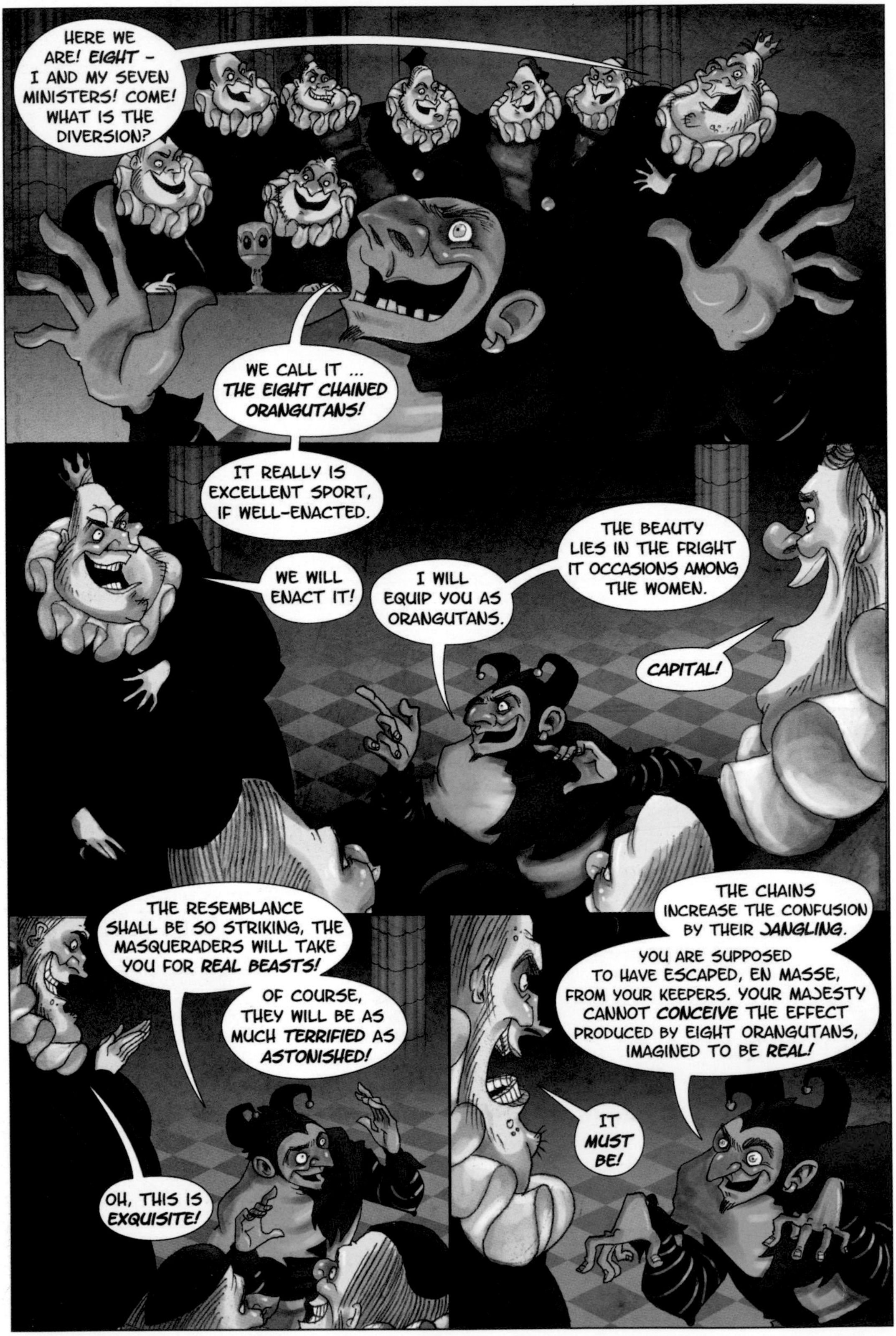
HERE WE ARE! EIGHT - I AND MY SEVEN MINISTERS! COME! WHAT IS THE DIVERSION?
WE CALL IT ... THE EIGHT CHAINED ORANGUTANS!
IT REALLY IS EXCELLENT SPORT, IF WELL-ENACTED.
WE WILL ENACT IT!
I WILL EQUIP YOU AS ORANGUTANS.
THE BEAUTY LIES IN THE FRIGHT IT OCCASIONS AMONG THE WOMEN.
CAPITAL!
THE RESEMBLANCE SHALL BE SO STRIKING, THE MASQUERADERS WILL TAKE YOU FOR REAL BEASTS!
OF COURSE, THEY WILL BE AS MUCH TERRIFIED AS ASTONISHED!
OH, THIS IS EXQUISITE!
THE CHAINS INCREASE THE CONFUSION BY THEIR JANGLING.
YOU ARE SUPPOSED TO HAVE ESCAPED, EN MASSE, FROM YOUR KEEPERS. YOUR MAJESTY CANNOT CONCEIVE THE EFFECT PRODUCED BY EIGHT ORANGUTANS, IMAGINED TO BE REAL!
IT MUST BE!

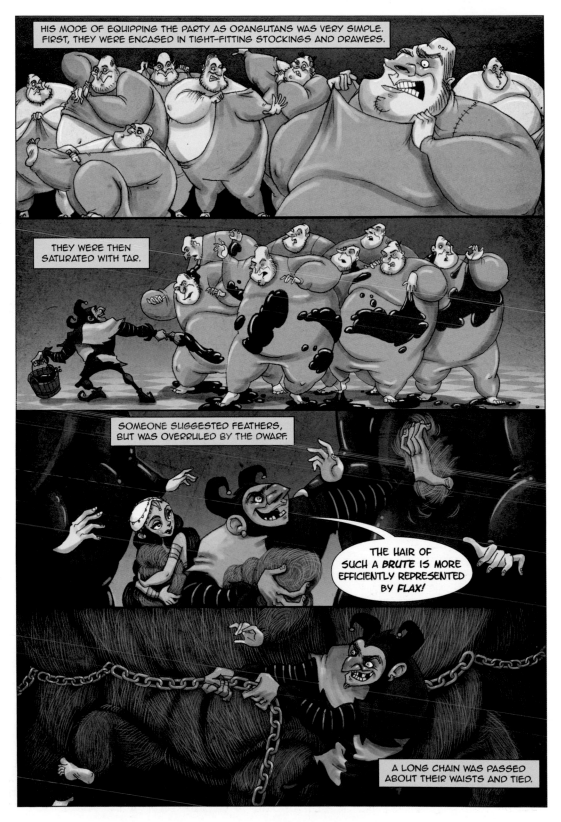

HIS MODE OF EQUIPPING THE PARTY AS ORANGUTANS WAS VERY SIMPLE. FIRST, THEY WERE ENCASED IN TIGHT-FITTING STOCKINGS AND DRAWERS.

THEY WERE THEN SATURATED WITH TAR.

SOMEONE SUGGESTED FEATHERS, BUT WAS OVERRULED BY THE DWARF.

THE HAIR OF SUCH A *BRUTE* IS MORE EFFICIENTLY REPRESENTED BY *FLAX!*

A LONG CHAIN WAS PASSED ABOUT THEIR WAISTS AND TIED.

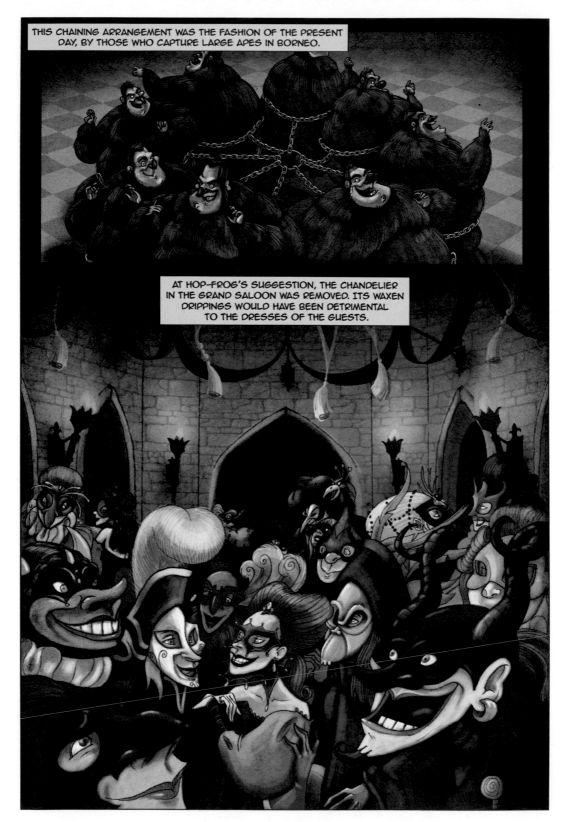

THIS CHAINING ARRANGEMENT WAS THE FASHION OF THE PRESENT DAY, BY THOSE WHO CAPTURE LARGE APES IN BORNEO.

AT HOP-FROG'S SUGGESTION, THE CHANDELIER IN THE GRAND SALOON WAS REMOVED. ITS WAXEN DRIPPINGS WOULD HAVE BEEN DETRIMENTAL TO THE DRESSES OF THE GUESTS.

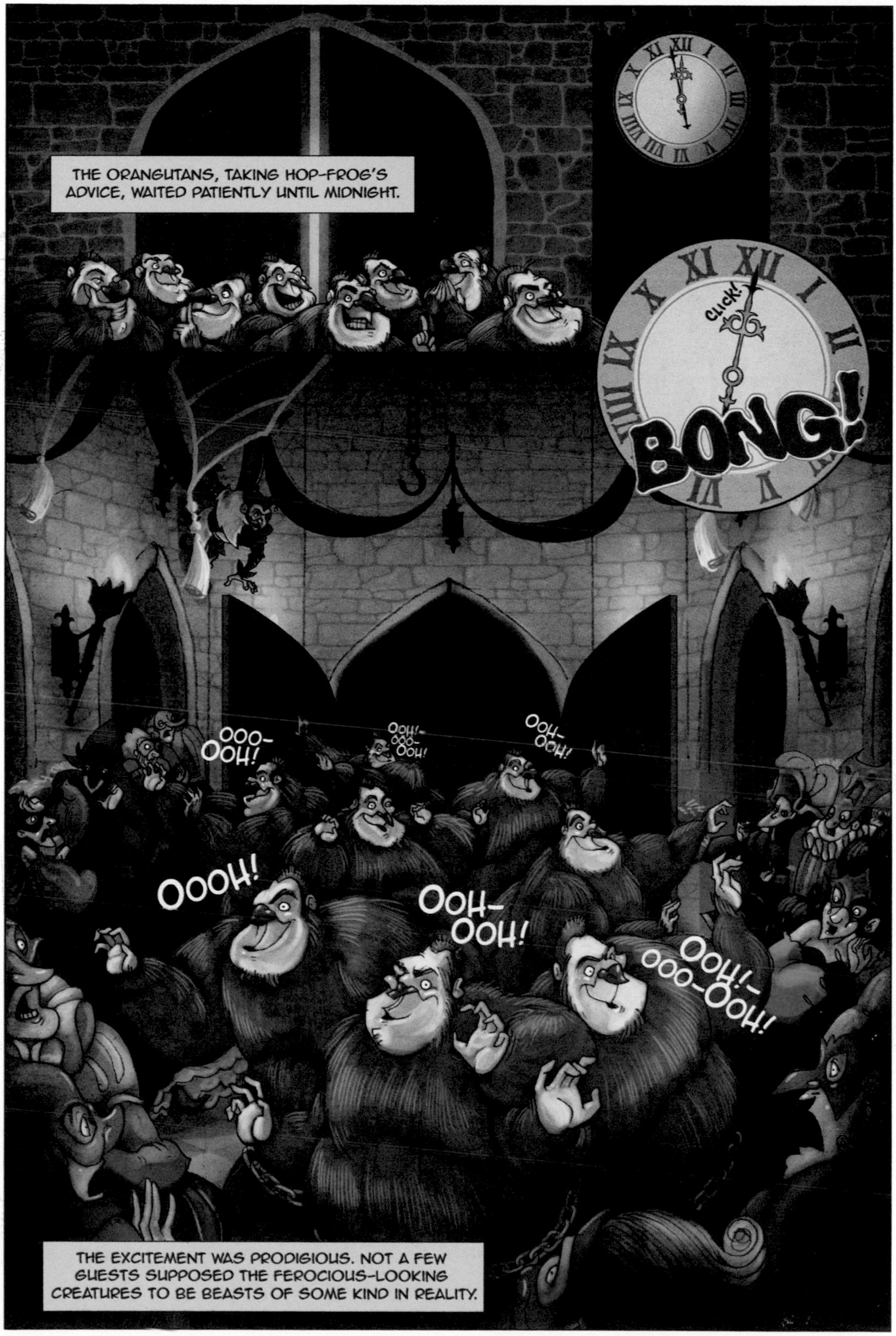
THE ORANGUTANS, TAKING HOP-FROG'S ADVICE, WAITED PATIENTLY UNTIL MIDNIGHT.
CLICK!
BONG!
OOO-OOH!
OOH!-OOO-OOH!
OOH-OOH!
OOOH!
OOH-OOH!
OOH!-OOO-OOO-OOH!
THE EXCITEMENT WAS PRODIGIOUS. NOT A FEW GUESTS SUPPOSED THE FEROCIOUS-LOOKING CREATURES TO BE BEASTS OF SOME KIND IN REALITY.

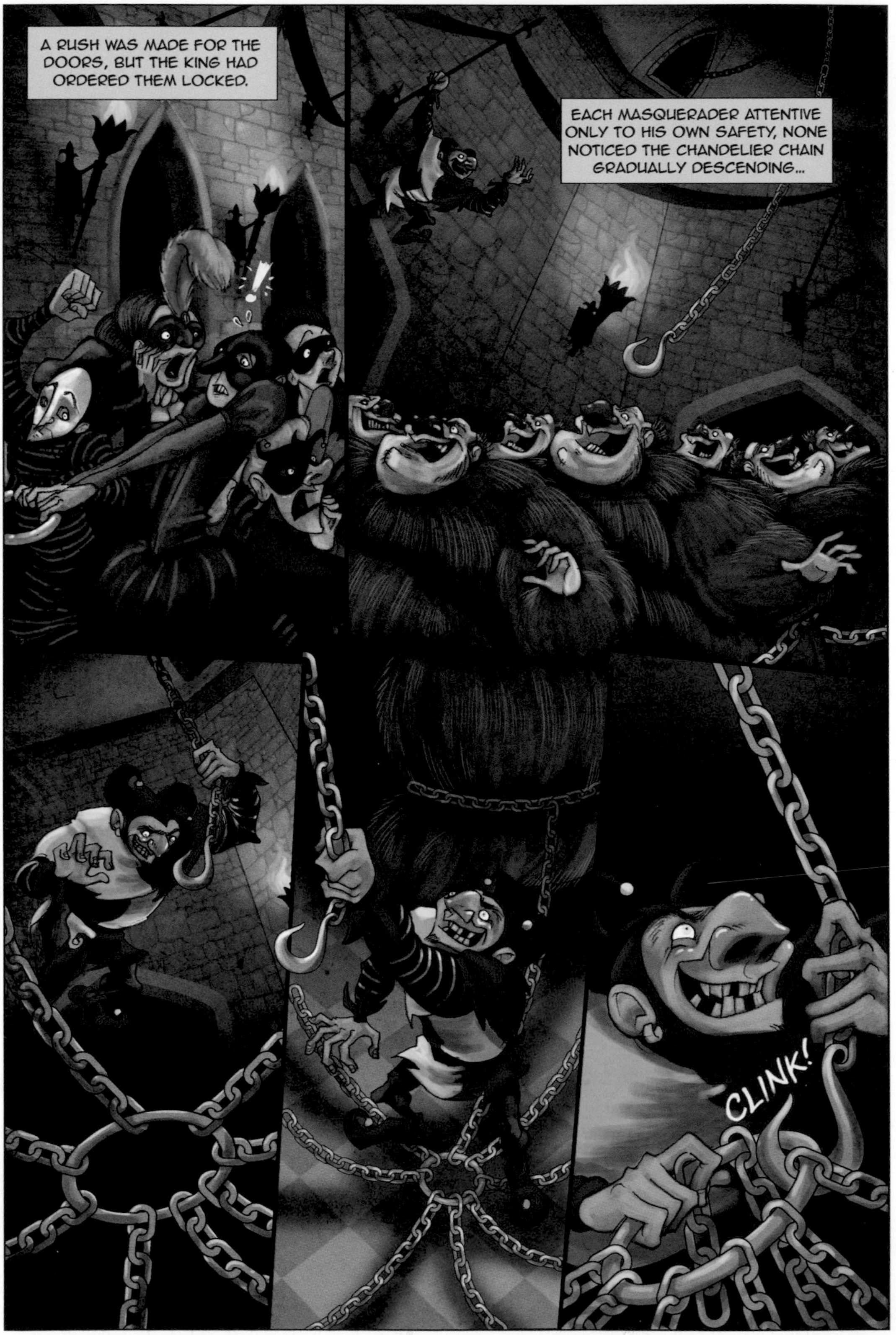
A RUSH WAS MADE FOR THE DOORS, BUT THE KING HAD ORDERED THEM LOCKED.
EACH MASQUERADER ATTENTIVE ONLY TO HIS OWN SAFETY, NONE NOTICED THE CHANDELIER CHAIN GRADUALLY DESCENDING...
CLINK!

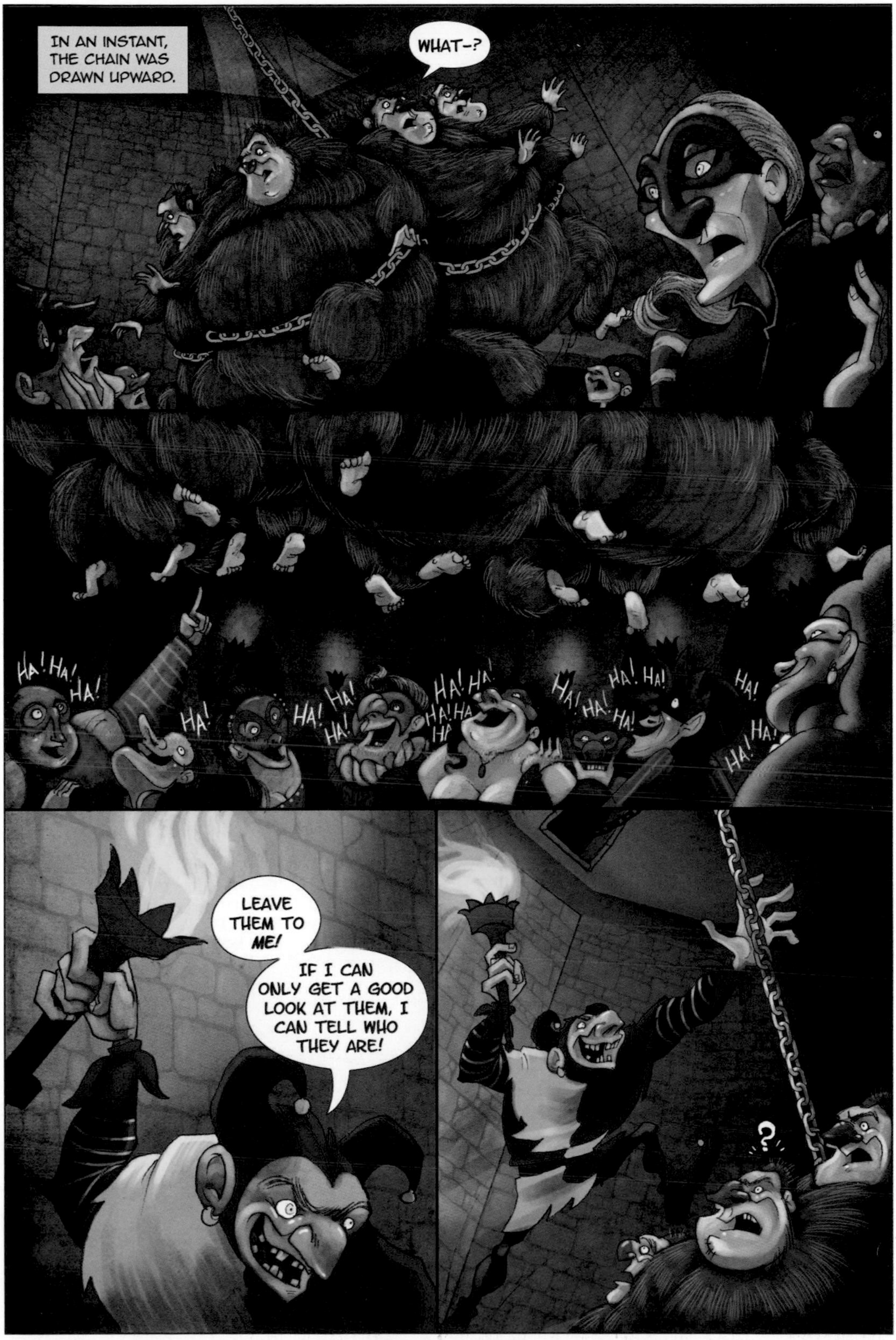
IN AN INSTANT, THE CHAIN WAS DRAWN UPWARD.
WHAT-?
HA! HA! HA!
HA!
HA!
HA!
HA! HA!
HA! HA!
HA! HA!
HA!
HA!
HA!
LEAVE THEM TO ME!
IF I CAN ONLY GET A GOOD LOOK AT THEM, I CAN TELL WHO THEY ARE!
?

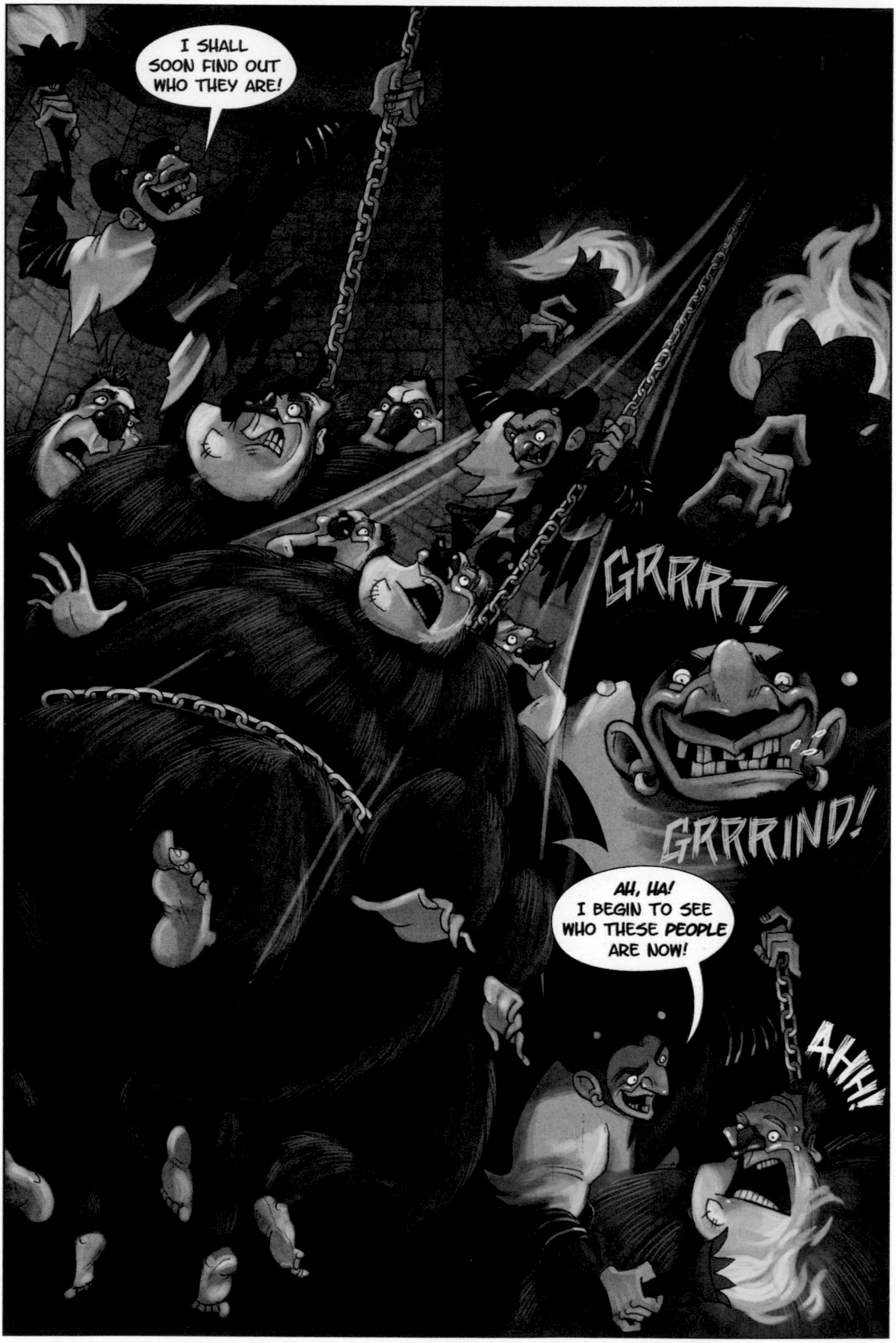
I SHALL SOON FIND OUT WHO THEY ARE!
GRRRT!
GRRRIND!
AH, HA! I BEGIN TO SEE WHO THESE PEOPLE ARE NOW!
AHHH!

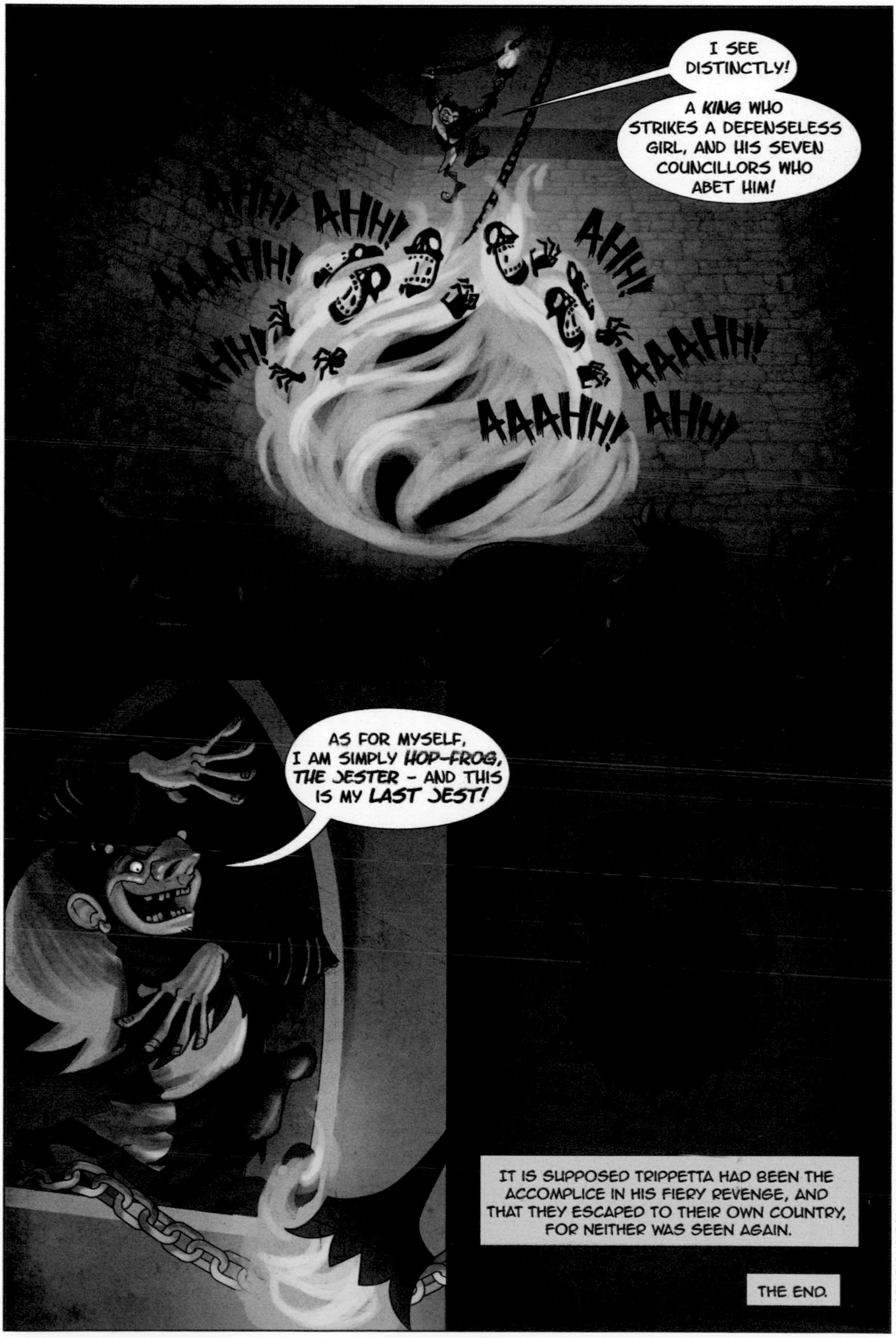
I SEE DISTINCTLY!
A KING WHO STRIKES A DEFENSELESS GIRL, AND HIS SEVEN COUNCILLORS WHO ABET HIM!
AHH! AAAHH! AHH! AHH! AAAHH! AAAHH! AHH!
AS FOR MYSELF, I AM SIMPLY HOP-FROG, THE JESTER - AND THIS IS MY LAST JEST!
IT IS SUPPOSED TRIPPETTA HAD BEEN THE ACCOMPLICE IN HIS FIERY REVENGE, AND THAT THEY ESCAPED TO THEIR OWN COUNTRY, FOR NEITHER WAS SEEN AGAIN.
THE END.

The Oval Portrait

ADAPTED BY
TOM POMPLUN
ILLUSTRATED BY
CRAIG WILSON

THE CHATEAU INTO WHICH MY VALET HAD VENTURED TO MAKE FORCIBLE ENTRANCE, RATHER THAN PERMIT ME, IN MY WEAKENED CONDITION, TO PASS A NIGHT IN THE OPEN AIR, WAS ONE OF THOSE PILES OF COMMINGLED GLOOM AND GRANDEUR WHICH HAVE SO LONG FROWNED AMONG THE APENNINES.

TO ALL APPEARANCE THE PLACE HAD BEEN TEMPORARILY AND VERY LATELY ABANDONED.

WE ESTABLISHED OURSELVES IN ONE OF THE SMALLEST AND LEAST SUMPTUOUSLY FURNISHED APARTMENTS. IT LAY IN A REMOTE TURRET OF THE BUILDING.

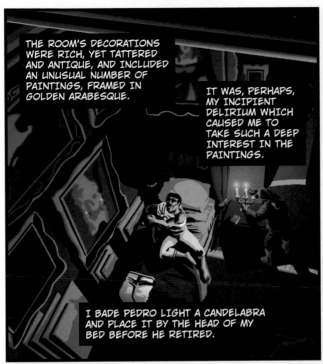

THE ROOM'S DECORATIONS WERE RICH, YET TATTERED AND ANTIQUE, AND INCLUDED AN UNUSUAL NUMBER OF PAINTINGS, FRAMED IN GOLDEN ARABESQUE.

IT WAS, PERHAPS, MY INCIPIENT DELIRIUM WHICH CAUSED ME TO TAKE SUCH A DEEP INTEREST IN THE PAINTINGS.

I BADE PEDRO LIGHT A CANDELABRA AND PLACE IT BY THE HEAD OF MY BED BEFORE HE RETIRED.

I WISHED TO RESIGN MYSELF, IF NOT TO SLEEP, AT LEAST ALTERNATELY TO THE CONTEMPLATION OF THE PICTURES...

...AND THE PERUSAL OF A SMALL VOLUME WHICH DESCRIBED THEM, AND WHICH I HAD FOUND NEXT TO THE BED.

LONG — LONG I READ — AND DEVOUTLY, DEVOTEDLY I GAZED, AS THE DEEP MIDNIGHT CAME AND MY VALET SLUMBERED IN PEACE.

WHEN, AT LENGTH, I ADJUSTED THE POSITION OF THE CANDELABRA TO FACILITATE MY READING, THE ACTION PRODUCED AN EFFECT ALTOGETHER UNANTICIPATED.

THE RAYS FELL WITHIN A NICHE OF THE ROOM WHICH HAD HITHERTO BEEN THROWN INTO DEEP SHADE, AND I THUS SAW IN VIVID LIGHT A PICTURE UNNOTICED BEFORE.

IT WAS THE PORTRAIT OF A YOUNG GIRL JUST RIPENING INTO WOMANHOOD.

THE FRAME WAS OVAL, RICHLY GILDED AND FILAGREED.

BUT IT WAS NEITHER THE EXECUTION OF THE WORK, NOR THE IMMORTAL BEAUTY OF THE COUNTENANCE, WHICH SO MOVED ME.

THE SPELL OF THE PICTURE WAS IN AN ABSOLUTE LIFE-LIKELINESS OF EXPRESSION, WHICH AT FIRST STARTLED, THEN CONFOUNDED, AND FINALLY APPALLED ME.

WITH DEEP AND REVERENT AWE, I TOOK UP THE VOLUME AND TURNED TO THE LAST ENTRY, WHICH DESCRIBED THE PORTRAIT.

"SHE WAS A MAIDEN OF RAREST BEAUTY, AND NOT MORE LOVELY THAN FULL OF GLEE. AND EVIL WAS THE HOUR WHEN SHE SAW, AND LOVED, AND WEDDED THE PAINTER."

"HE, PASSIONATE, STUDIOUS, AUSTERE, AND HAVING ALREADY A BRIDE IN HIS ART."

"SHE ALL LIGHT AND SMILES, AND LOVING AND CHERISHING ALL THINGS — HATING ONLY THE ART WHICH WAS HER RIVAL."

"IT WAS THUS A TERRIBLE THING FOR THIS LADY TO HEAR OF THE PAINTER'S DESIRE TO PORTRAY EVEN HIS BRIDE. BUT SHE SAT MEEKLY FOR MANY WEEKS IN THE HIGH TURRET-CHAMBER."

"THE PAINTER'S WORK WENT ON FROM HOUR TO HOUR AND FROM DAY TO DAY. HE COULD NOT SEE THE WITHERED HEALTH AND SPIRITS OF HIS BRIDE."

"YET SHE SMILED ON, AND GREW DAILY MORE DISPIRITED AND WEAK."

"AS THE LABOR DREW NEARER CONCLUSION, THE PAINTER GREW WILD WITH THE ARDOR OF HIS WORK, AND TURNED HIS EYES FROM THE CANVAS RARELY, EVEN TO REGARD THE COUNTENANCE OF HIS WIFE."

"AND WHEN MANY WEEKS HAD PASSED, THE FINAL STROKE AT LAST WAS PLACED."

"THE PAINTER STOOD ENTRANCED BEFORE THE WORK WHICH HE HAD WROUGHT."

THIS IS, INDEED, LIFE ITSELF!

"BUT WHILE HE YET GAZED HE GREW AGHAST."

"HE TURNED SUDDENLY TO REGARD HIS BELOVED —"

"SHE WAS DEAD!"

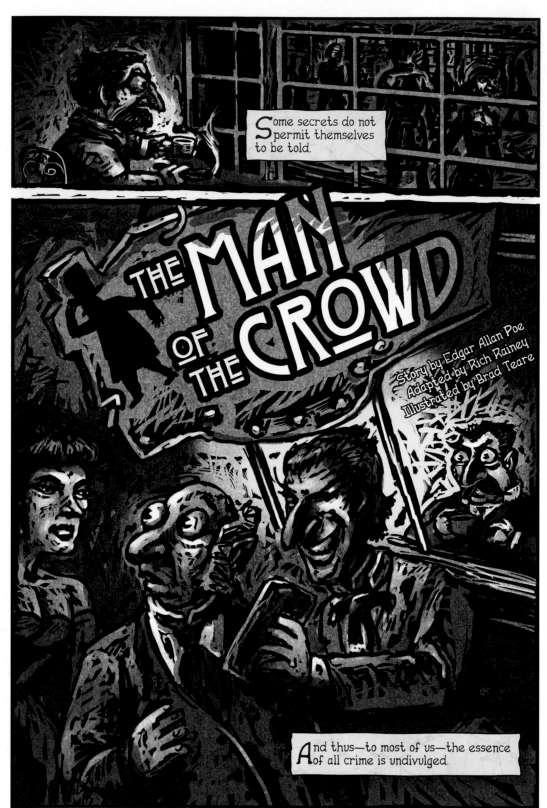

Some secrets do not permit themselves to be told.

THE MAN OF THE CROWD

Story by Edgar Allan Poe
Adapted by Rich Rainey
Illustrated by Brad Teare

And thus—to most of us—the essence of all crime is undivulged.

It was an autumn evening not long ago, when after months of ill health I felt a calm but inquisitive interest in everything. Merely to breathe was enjoyment.

And I derived positive pleasure even from many legitimate sources of pain.

I amused myself for most of the afternoon at the coffee-house window of the Delamar Hotel in London, peering out onto the street, observing the promiscuous company in the room...

...And studying the advertisements in the paper.

As darkness drew near, I became absorbed in contemplating the increasing tides of population that rushed by my window.

Mostly junior clerks from flash houses...Now and then an upper clerk from a staunch firm, his right ear bent sharply from years of having a pen tucked behind it.

The nature of the crowd altered as night deepened, with gamblers wearing everything from velvet jackets to clerical collars to make them look less suspicious.

Modest young girls return-ing from a long day's labor, shrinking from a ruffian's glances.

Coquettish women parading themselves to the crowd.

Countless drunkards in shreds and patches, reeling and inarticulate.

With my brow to the glass, there suddenly came into view an old man who absorbed my whole attention.

His countenance seemed greater than any of Retzch's paintings of the devil himself.

From him came a paradoxical sense of power and caution, coolness and malice, triumph and terror. And supreme despair.

How wild a history was written in that bosom?

There came a craving desire to keep the man in view.

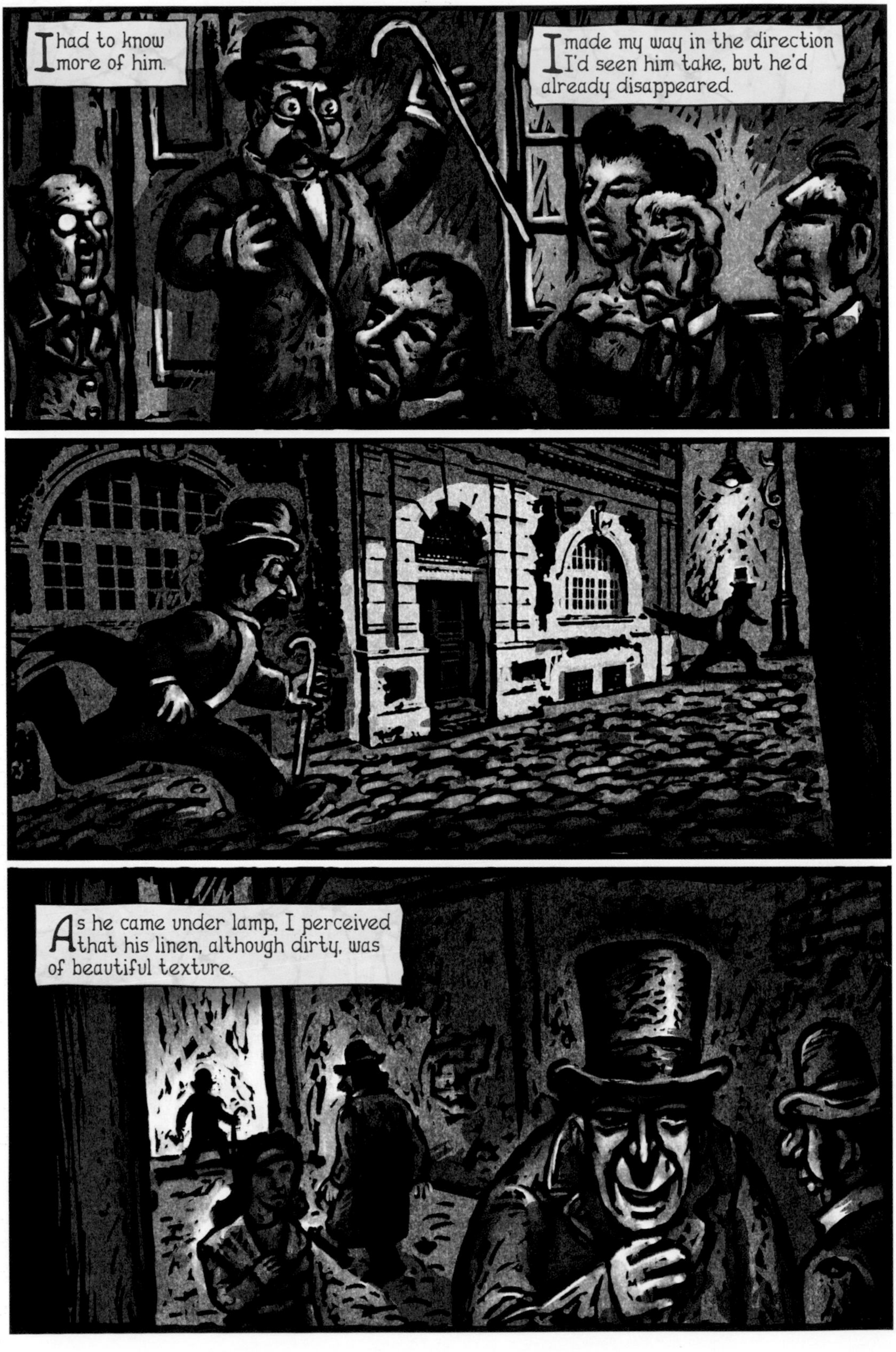
I had to know more of him.
I made my way in the direction I'd seen him take, but he'd already disappeared.
As he came under lamp, I perceived that his linen, although dirty, was of beautiful texture.

Well suited for a man once accustomed to weapons and to wealth.

I resolved to follow the stranger wherever he went.

Beneath the rent in his second-hand vest I glimpsed a diamond and dagger.

For half an hour the old man held his way with difficulty along the great thoroughfare.

At times I walked close at his elbow through fear of losing sight of him.

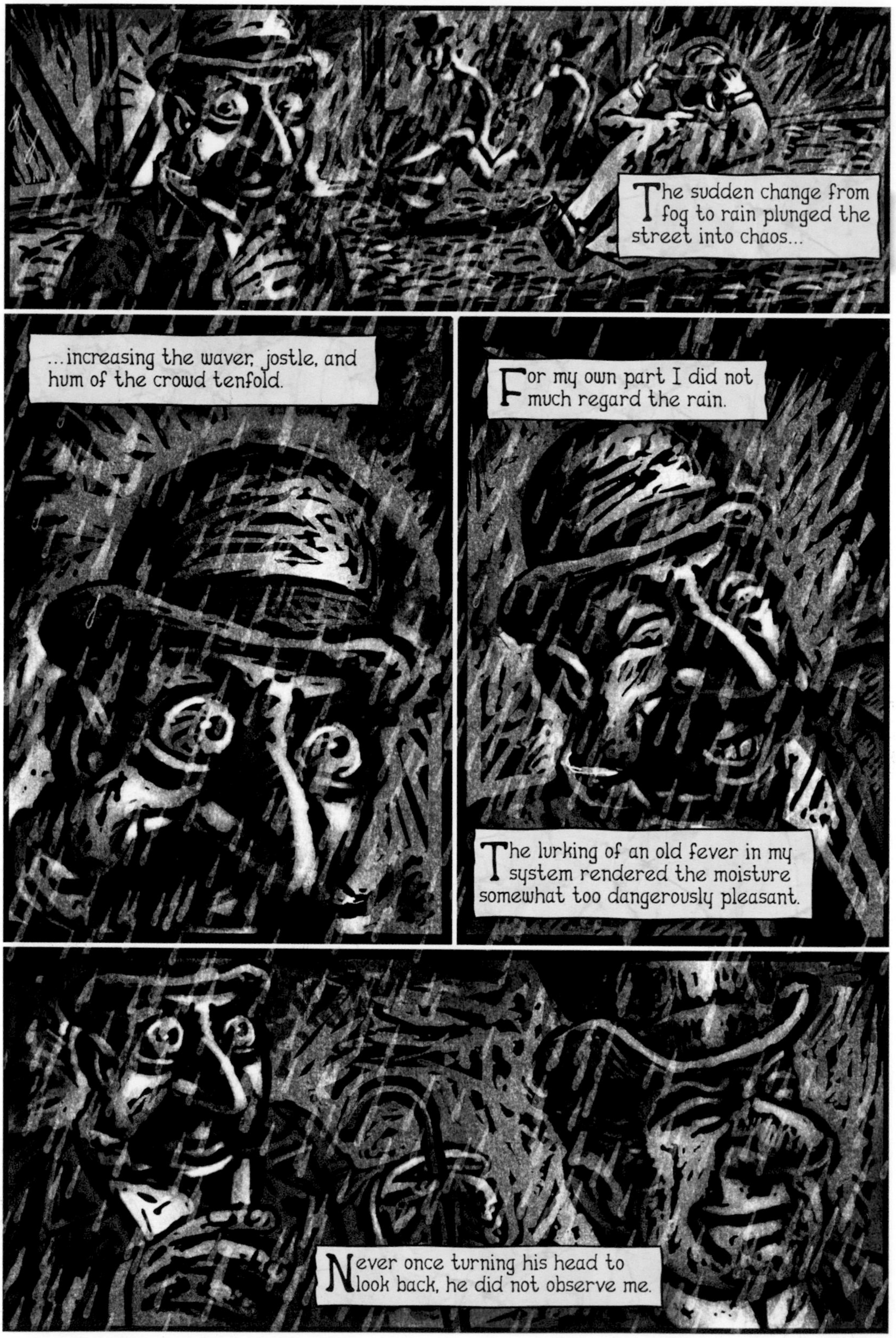
The sudden change from fog to rain plunged the street into chaos...
...increasing the waver, jostle, and hum of the crowd tenfold.
For my own part I did not much regard the rain.
The lurking of an old fever in my system rendered the moisture somewhat too dangerously pleasant.
Never once turning his head to look back, he did not observe me.

When he deserted the main street for a less crowded thoroughfare his demeanor changed.

He walked more slowly and with less object than before

Crossing and re-crossing the street without apparent aim for nearly an hour.

When his next turn brought us to a square overflowing with life, the manner of the stranger returned.

His eyes rolled wildly upon those who hemmed him in. He urged his way steadily and perseveringly.

Upon his having made the circuit of the square, he retraced his steps.

I was astonished to see him repeat the same walk several times.

And once, he nearly detected me as he came round with a sudden movement.

In this exercise he spent another hour, at the end of which we met with far less interruption from passengers than at first.

The rain fell fast, the air grew cool, and the people were retiring to their homes.

The wanderer rushed into a nearly empty bye-street, moving faster than I could have dreamed from one so aged.

It greatly troubled my pursuit...

Until we passed into a bazaar the stranger appeared well acquainted with.

During the hour we passed in this place he entered shop after shop, priced nothing, spoke no word.

He looked at all objects with a wild and vacant stare. Amazed at his behavior, I resolved we would not part until I satisfied myself in some measure respecting him.

It required caution to stay within reach without attracting his observation. Luckily the overshoes I wore allowed me to move in perfect silence.

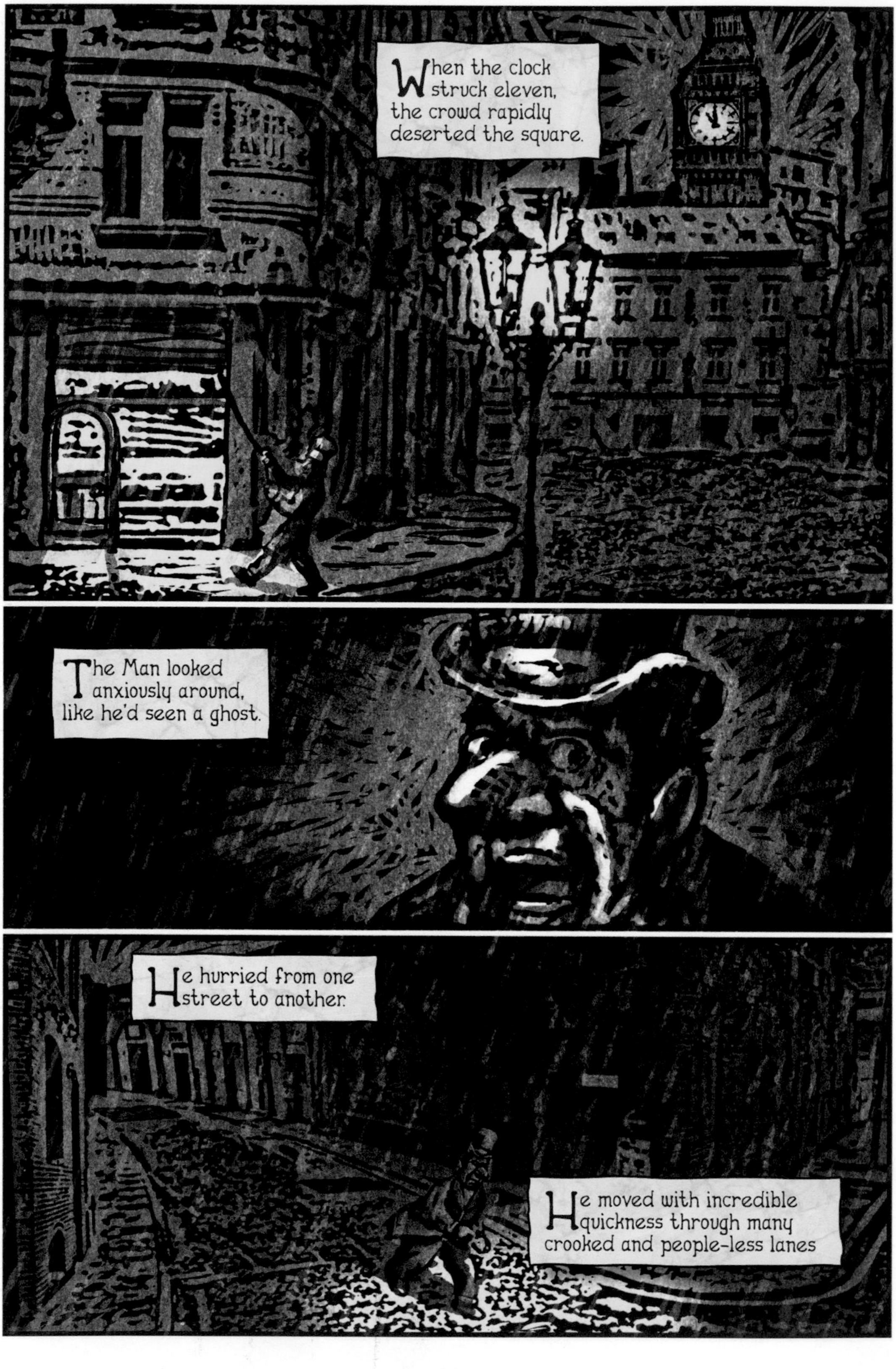
When the clock struck eleven, the crowd rapidly deserted the square.
The Man looked anxiously around, like he'd seen a ghost.
He hurried from one street to another.
He moved with incredible quickness through many crooked and people-less lanes

Until we emerged once more upon the great thoroughfare whence we had started.

The street of the Delamar Hotel.

It was still brilliant with gaslight but few persons were seen.

The Man grew pale, walked moodily up the once populous avenue. With a sigh he turned a corner and led us a variety of ways until—

At last we came in view of one of the principal theaters.

The agony on his face abated as he followed a party of roisterers.

But they dropped off one by one until only a few remained in a little-frequented lane.

He paused lost in thought. Then, as sudden inspiration seized him...

He turned and pursued a route to the verge of the city.

It was home to the most deplorable poverty and desperate crime.

A blaze of light burst upon us and we stood before a huge temple, a palace of the fiend, GIN.

With a shriek of joy, he went into the throng and was sated with activity once again...

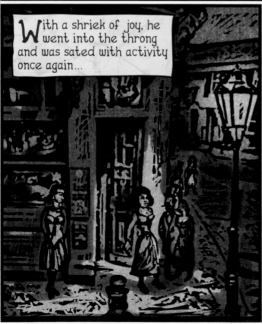

Until the dawn came, the doors closed, and the revelers retreated to their warrens.

With a mad energy, the man spun around...

...and retraced his steps to the heart of London.

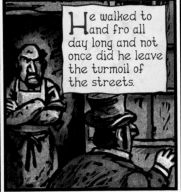

He walked to and fro all day long and not once did he leave the turmoil of the streets.

And as the shades of the second evening came on...

...I grew wearied unto death.

Stopping fully in front of the wanderer, I gazed steadfastly at his face.

But he noticed me not, resuming his solemn walk while I remained absorbed in thought.

This man is the type and the genius of deep crime. He refuses to be alone. He is the man of the crowd and it will be vain to follow.

I can learn no more of him or his deeds. For some secrets do not permit themselves to be told.

THE END

93

Spirits of the Dead

by EDGAR ALLAN POE

illustrated by ANDY EWEN / color by BENJAMIN WRIGHT

Thy soul shall find itself alone
'Mid dark thoughts of the grey tomb-stone;
Not one, of all the crowd, to pry
Into thine hour of secrecy.

Be silent in that solitude,
Which is not loneliness—for then
The spirits of the dead who stood
In life before thee are again
In death around thee, and their will
Shall then overshadow thee: be still.

For the night, though clear, shall frown,
And the stars shall look not down
From their high thrones in the Heaven
With light like hope to mortals given,
But their red orbs, without beam,
To thy weariness shall seem
As a burning and a fever
Which would cling to thee for ever.

Now are thoughts thou shalt not banish,
Now are visions ne'er to vanish;
From thy spirit shall they pass
No more, like dew-drop from the grass.

The breeze, the breath of God, is still,
And the mist upon the hill
Shadowy, shadowy, yet unbroken,
Is a symbol and a token.
How it hangs upon the trees,
A mystery of mysteries!

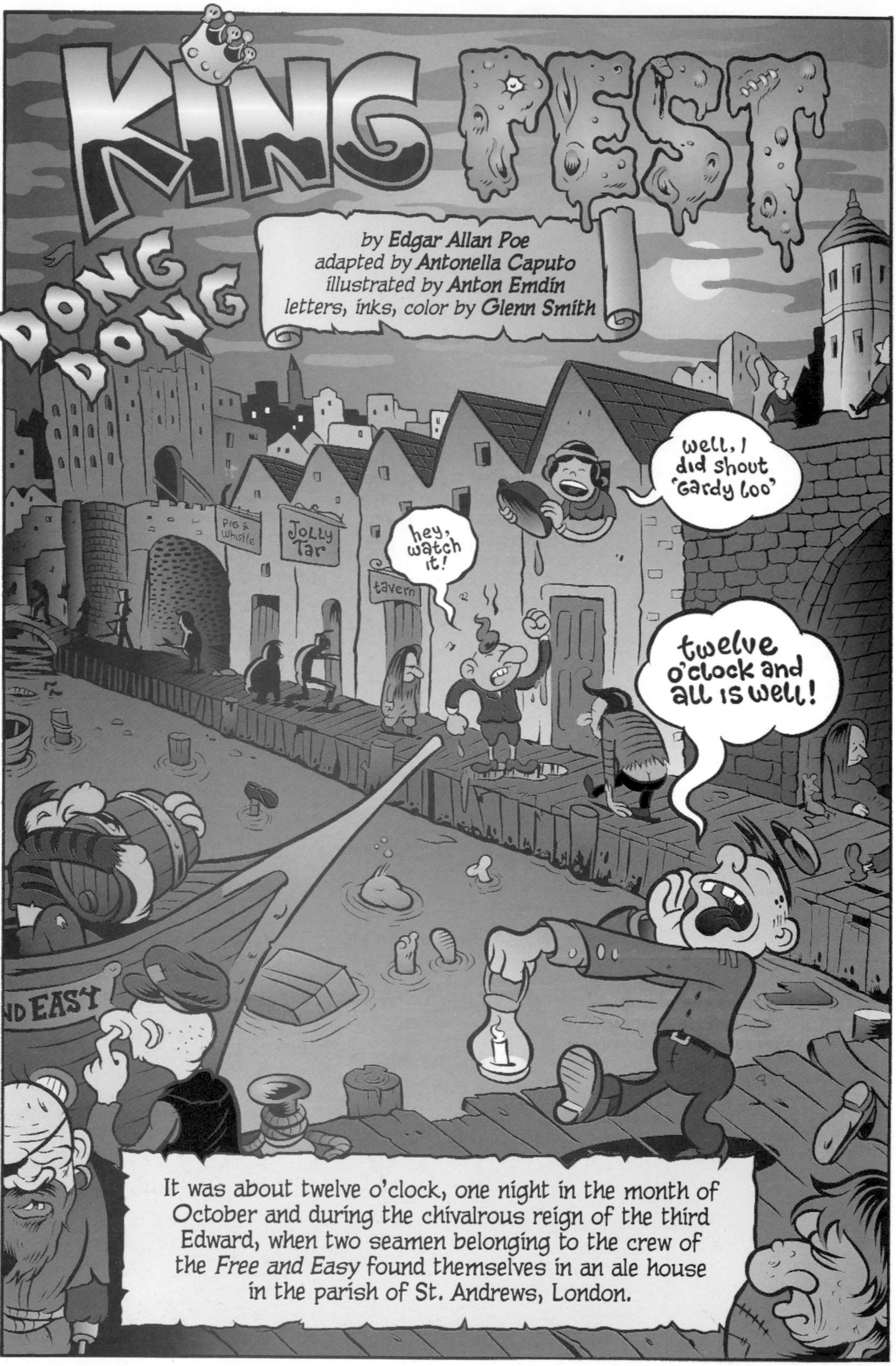
KING PEST
by Edgar Allan Poe
adapted by Antonella Caputo
illustrated by Anton Emdin
letters, inks, color by Glenn Smith
DONG DONG
PIG & Whistle
Jolly Tar
tavern
hey, watch it!
well, I did shout 'Gardy Loo'
twelve o'clock and all is well!
ND EASY
It was about twelve o'clock, one night in the month of October and during the chivalrous reign of the third Edward, when two seamen belonging to the crew of the *Free and Easy* found themselves in an ale house in the parish of St. Andrews, London.

Various had been the peregrinations of the worthy couple in and about the different tap-houses.

It was with empty pockets our friends had ventured upon the present hostelrie.

They were eyeing, from behind a huge flagon of unpaid-for 'humming-stuff', a sign conspicuously hung above the establishment's door.

It seems that our **credit** will not suffice here.

aye, I fear this omen forbodes a long run of **dirty weather!**

then I believe it is time to **pump ship**, clew up all sail, and **scud** before the wind!

97

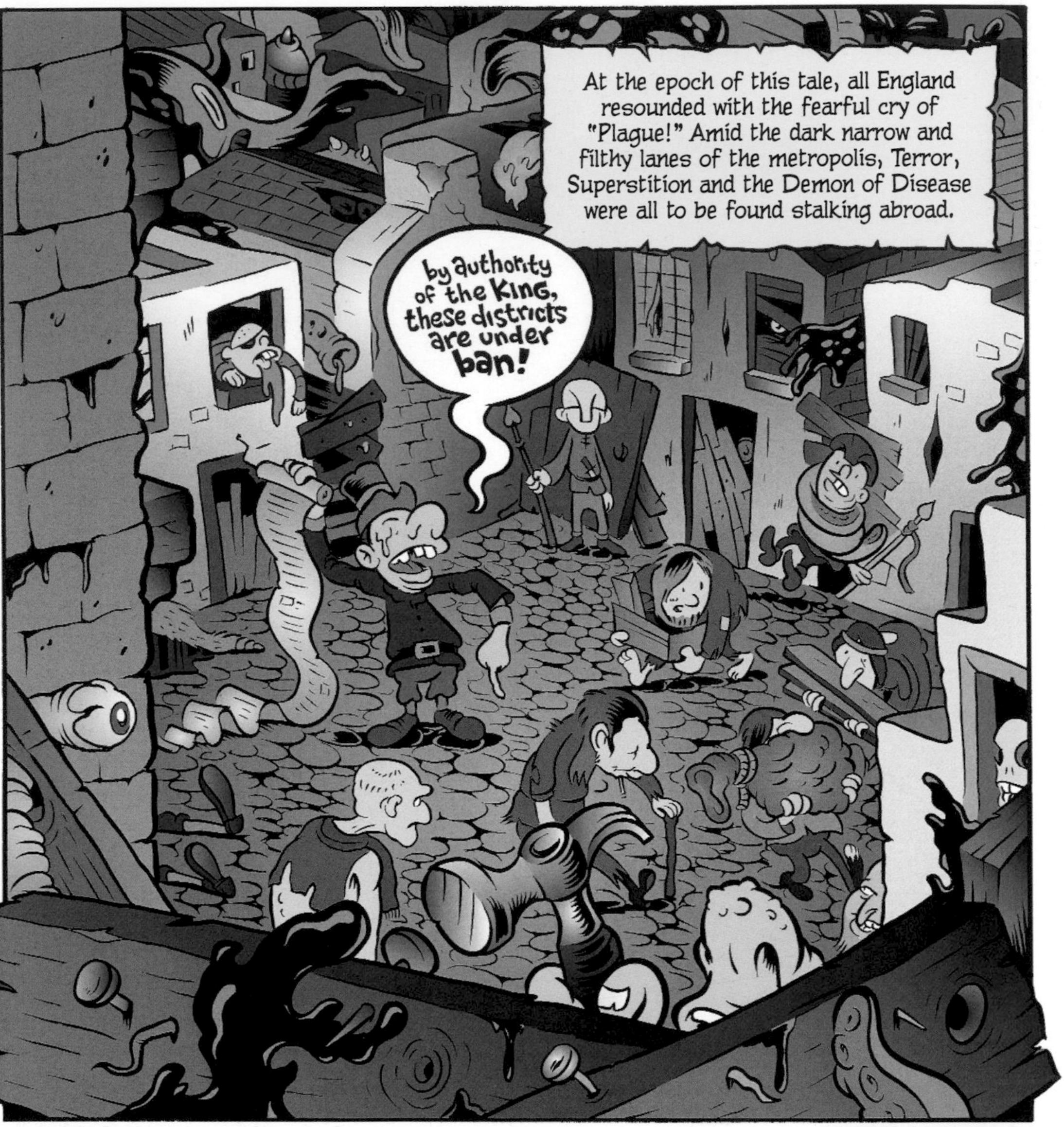
At the epoch of this tale, all England resounded with the fearful cry of "Plague!" Amid the dark narrow and filthy lanes of the metropolis, Terror, Superstition and the Demon of Disease were all to be found stalking abroad.
by authority of the King, these districts are under ban!

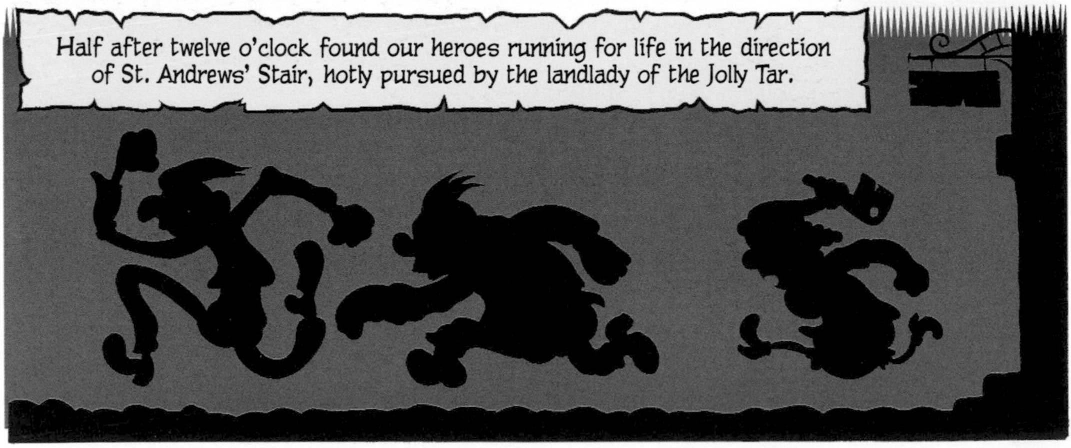
Half after twelve o'clock found our heroes running for life in the direction of St. Andrews' Stair, hotly pursued by the landlady of the Jolly Tar.

Neither the mandate of the monarch, nor the huge barriers, nor the prospect of that loathsome death, prevented the nightly looting of the dwellings. But few of the terror-stricken people attributed these doings to the agency of human hands.

STORE

Pest-spirits, plague goblins, fever demons were the popular culprits; the plunderer himself was often scared away by the horrors his own depreciations had created.

Stop right there!

that alley is **banned**!

Stay back! there is **PLAGUE** in there!

It was by one of the terrific barriers that Legs and Hugh Tarpaulin found their progress suddenly impeded. But their pursuers were close, and to return was out of the question.

Had they not been intoxicated beyond moral sense, their reeling footsteps might have been palsied by the horrors of their situation.

The most fetid and poisonous smell everywhere prevailed. The carcass of many a nocturnal plunderer lay about, arrested by the hand of the plague in the very perpetration of his robbery.

But it lay not in the power of images to stay the course of men who, brimful of courage and of "humming-stuff", would have reeled, as straight as their condition permitted, into the very jaws of death.

forward, my friend!

Spirits beware! HAW HAW HAW

Suddenly, as the seamen stumbled against the entrance of a tall building, the shrill demand of Legs was replied to from within by a succession of fiendish shrieks.

Open, cries the Wolf!! HOWL!!!

So says his Demon companion! yak yak yak

Nothing daunted at the sounds which might have curdled the blood in hearts less irrevocably on fire, the drunken couple rushed headlong against the door and staggered into the midst of things.

arrrGGGhh..

CRASH!

a wine cellar! this bears INVESTIGATION!

Damnation! It's an undertaker's shop!

Look over there! a trap door!

er..Legs...

101

The apparent leader of the strange collective smiled graciously upon the intruders and offered them seats. He was a tall and emaciated man, with a forehead so unusually prominent as to have the appearance of a bonnet of flesh superadded upon his natural head.

take a **seat**, Gentlemen.

cheers!

with pleasure, my lord.

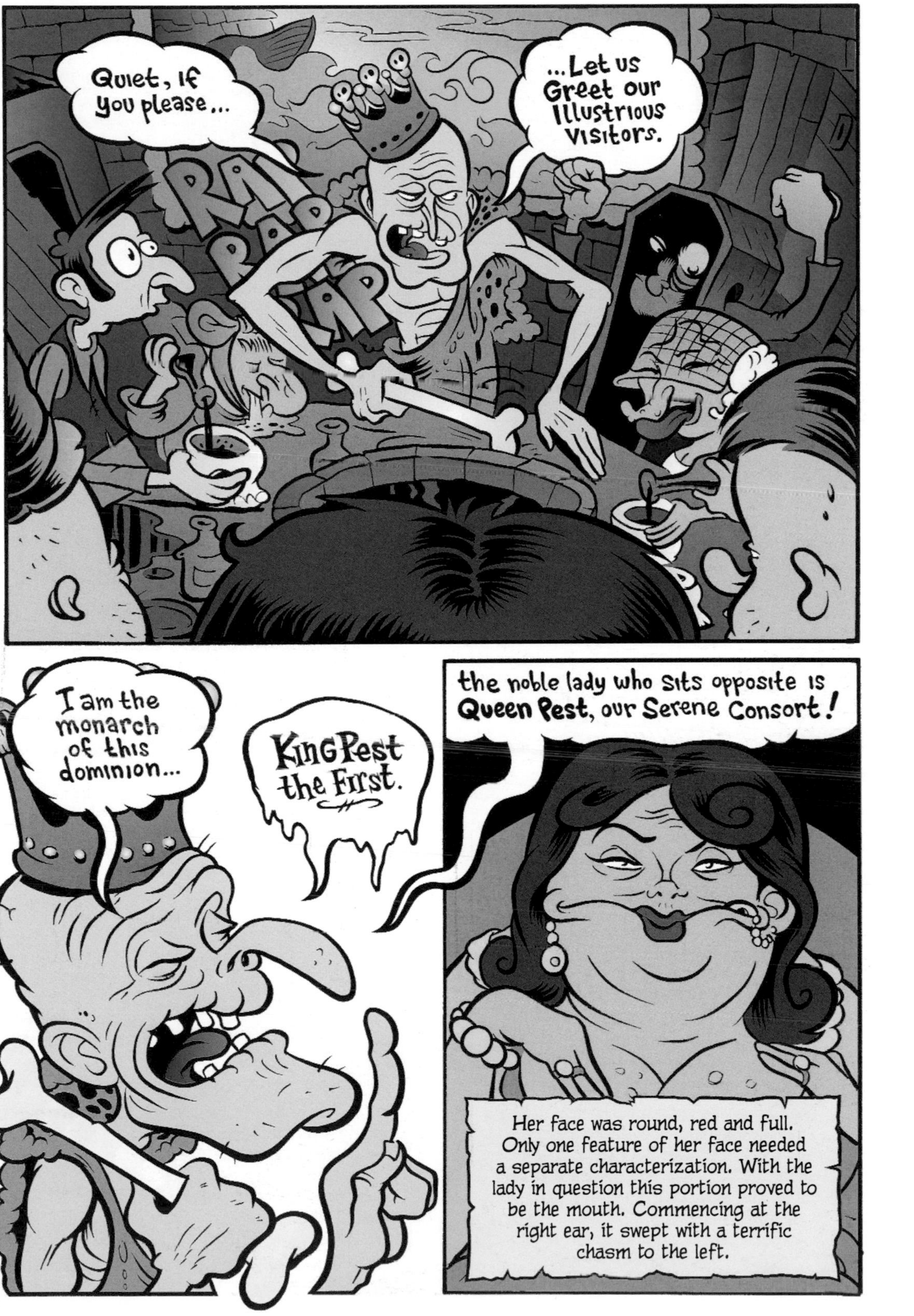
Quiet, if you please...
...Let us Greet our Illustrious visitors.
I am the monarch of this dominion...
King Pest the First.
the noble lady who sits opposite is Queen Pest, our Serene Consort!
Her face was round, red and full. Only one feature of her face needed a separate characterization. With the lady in question this portion proved to be the mouth. Commencing at the right ear, it swept with a terrific chasm to the left.

His Grace, the Arch Duke Pest-Iferous!

He was a puffy, wheezing and gouty old man, whose cheeks reposed upon the shoulders of their owner. He evidently prided much upon his gaudy coloured surcoat. This was made to fit him well, being fashioned from one of the silken covers which in England are customarily hung upon a conspicous wall.

His Grace, the Duke Pest-Ilential!

This gentleman's jaws were tightly tied up with a bandage, and his arms were fastened in a similar way, to prevent him from helping himself too freely to the liquors upon the table. A pair of prodigious ears towered away into the atmosphere of the apartment.

His Grace, the Duke of Tem-Pest!

The Duke was a singularly stiff-looking personage, who, being afflicted with paralysis, was habited in a new mahogany coffin. Arm-holes had been cut in the side, but the dress prevented its proprietor from sitting, and he lay reclining at an angle of forty-five degrees.

And finally, her Serene Highness, the Arch Duchess Ana-Pest!

The slight hectic spot which tinged the lady's leaden complexion, gave evident indication of a galloping consumption. Her nose, extremely long, thin, flexible and pimpled, hung down far below her under lip and she continually moved it from one side to the other with her tongue.

Avast there I say! Tell us what business ye have here...

...rigged off like foul fiends and swilling the snug blue ruin stowed away for the winter by my honest shipmate, Will Wimble the undertaker..!!

how dare you!

this is an offense!

I don't know you, sir!

you ar insole

Quiet! Please...Quiet!

At this unpardonable piece of ill-breeding, all the company started to their feet. The King was the first to recover his composure.

This apartment which you **profanely** suggest to be the shop of Will Wimble the undertaker, is the Dais-Chamber of our Palace, devoted to the councils of our **kingdom**!

As regards your demand of the business upon which we sit here in council, it concerns our own **private** and **regal** interest, and is therefore in no manner important to any other than ourselves!

105

But we will explain that we are here this night to examine, analyze and thoroughly determine the incomprehensible nature of those inestimable treasures of the palate: the wines, ales and liqueurs of this Goodly metropolis...

...and by so doing to advance, not more our own designs, than the true welfare of that unearthly Sovereign whose name is Death!

~Whose name is Davey Jones..!

tee hee

Profane varlet! Profane and execrable wretch! We have condescended to make reply to thy rude enquiries..!

Oops! hee hee

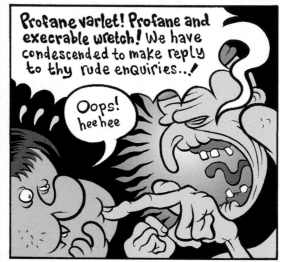

We nevertheless believe it our duty to penalize thee and thy companion each with a Gallon of Black Strap.

Having imbibed it as a single draught ye shall be free either to proceed upon your way or remain and be admitted to the privilege of our table.

It would be an **utter impossibility** to stow away in my hold even one-fourth part of the liquor you mentioned, for I already have a **full cargo.**

You will, your majesty, be so good as to take the **will** for the deed, for neither can I, nor will I, swallow another drop of the **villainous bilge-water** that answers to the name of **'Black Strap'!**

Belay that, you **lubber!** My hull is still **light!**

And as for the matter of your share of the cargo, why, rather than raise a squall I would **find stowage room** for it **myself!**

This proceeding is by **no means** in accordance with the **penalty,** which is not to be altered or recalled.

The condition we have imposed must be fulfilled to the **letter!** In failure of which we decree that you do here be tied neck and heels together and **drowned as rebels** in yon hogshead of **October beer!**

107

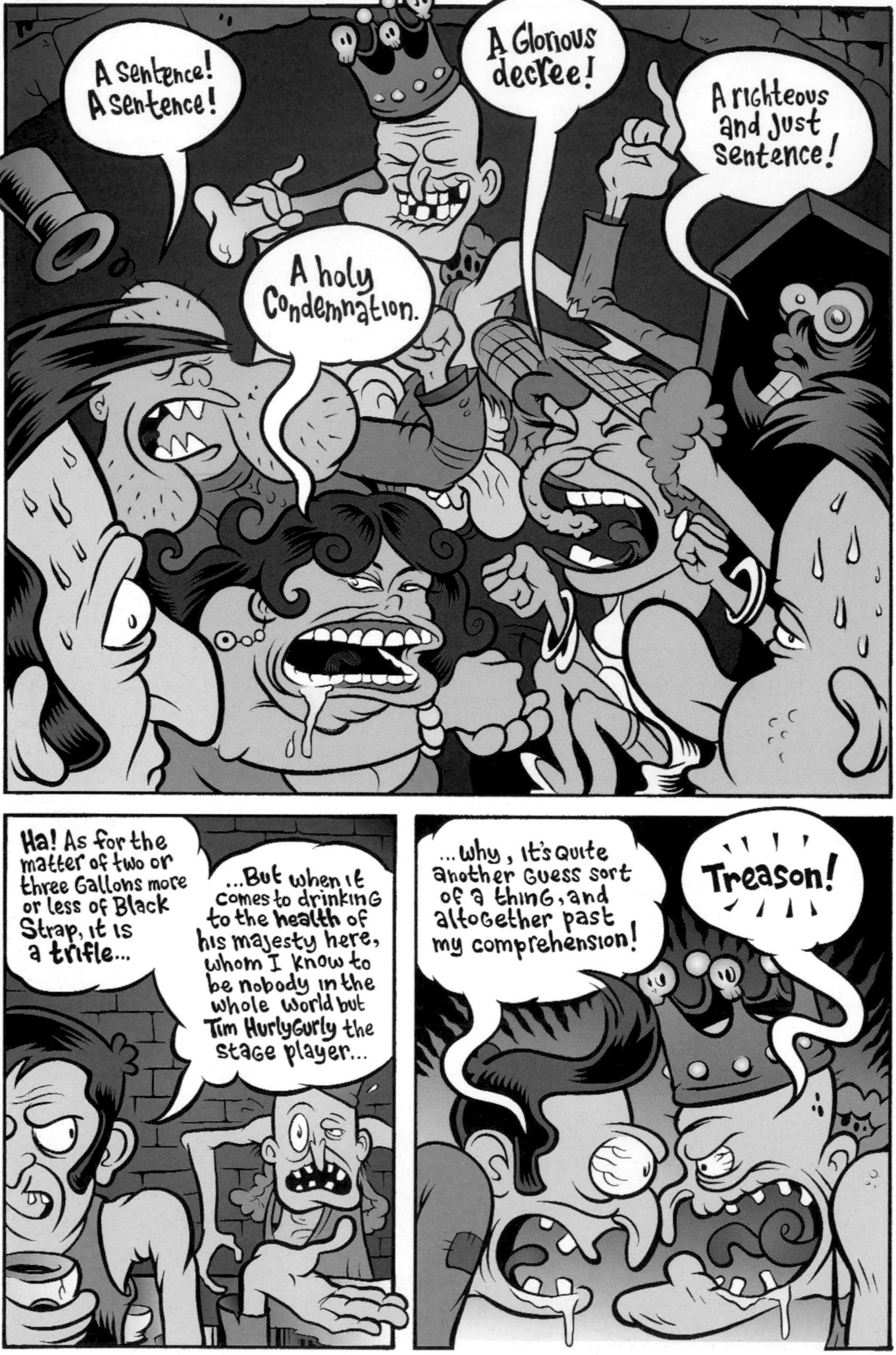
A sentence! A sentence!
A Glorious decree!
A righteous and just sentence!
A holy Condemnation.
Ha! As for the matter of two or three Gallons more or less of Black Strap, it is a trifle...
...But when it comes to drinking to the health of his majesty here, whom I know to be nobody in the whole world but Tim HurlyGurly the stage player...
...why, it's quite another Guess sort of a thing, and altogether past my comprehension!
Treason!

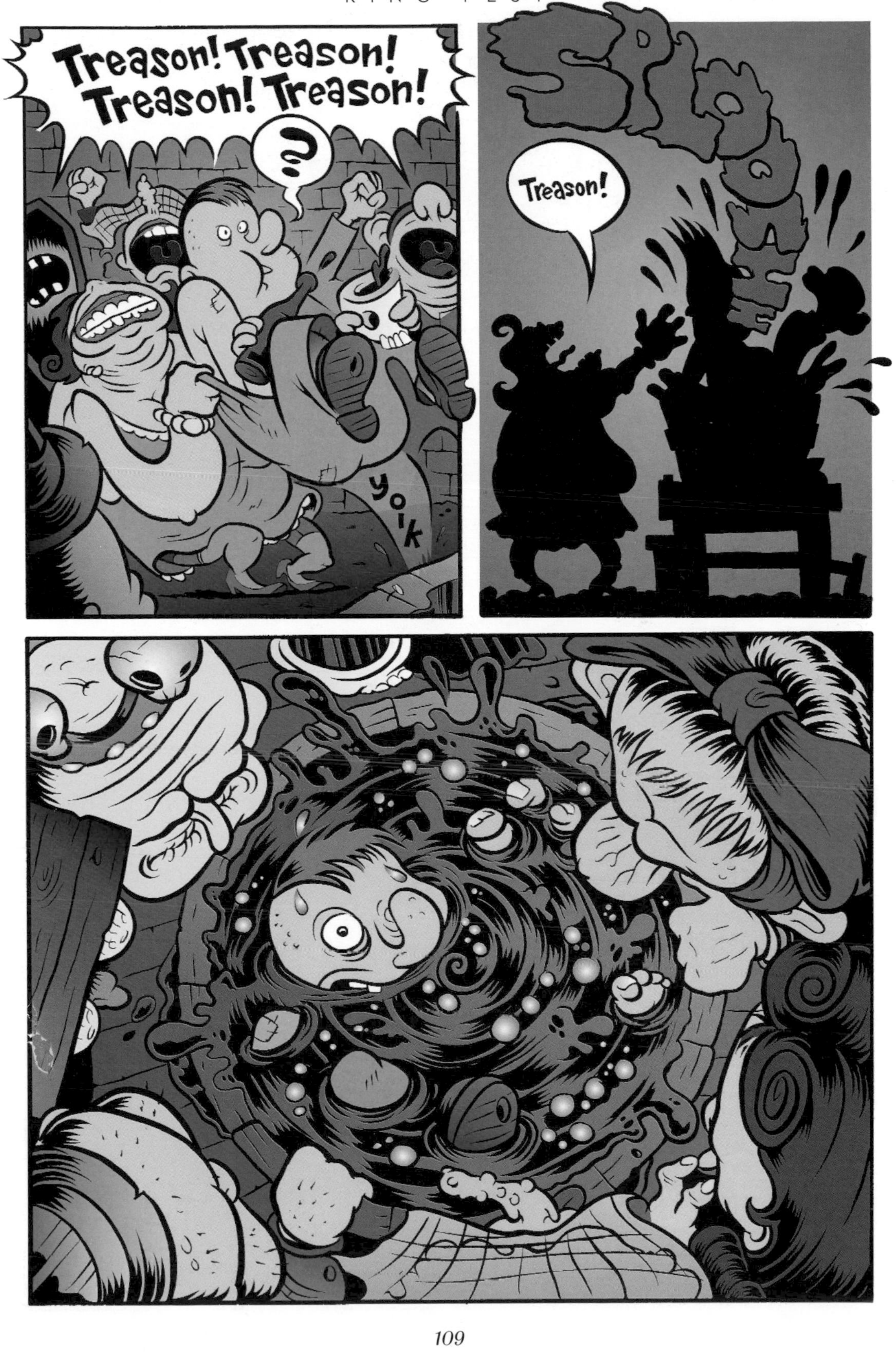
Treason! Treason!
Treason! Treason!
?
YOIK
Treason!

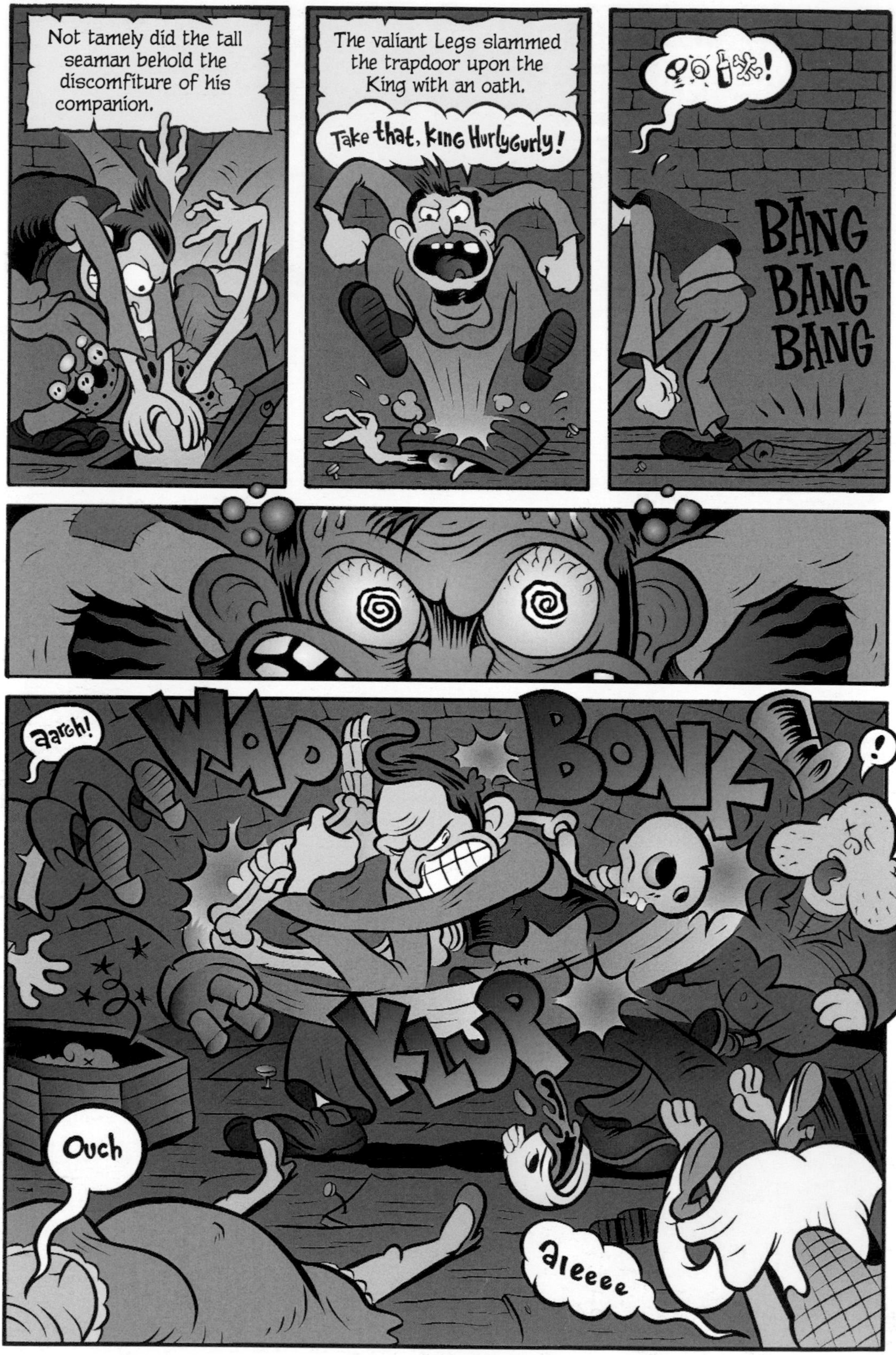
Not tamely did the tall seaman behold the discomfiture of his companion.
The valiant Legs slammed the trapdoor upon the King with an oath.
Take that, King HurlyGurly!
BANG
BANG
BANG
aargh!
WAP
BONK
!
KLUP
Ouch
aleeee

Out burst a deluge of liquor so fierce that the room was flooded from wall to wall.

The victorious Legs, seizing by the waist the fat lady, rushed out with her onto the street...

... followed by Hugh Tarpaulin with the Arch Duchess, as they made a bee-line for the *Free and Easy*.

The Tell-Tale Heart

TRUE! — NERVOUS, VERY, VERY DREADFULLY NERVOUS I HAD BEEN AND AM; BUT WHY WILL YOU SAY THAT I AM **MAD?** THE DISEASE HAD **SHARPENED** MY SENSES — NOT DESTROYED, NOT DULLED THEM. ABOVE ALL WAS MY SENSE OF HEARING ACUTE. I HEARD ALL THINGS IN HEAVEN AND EARTH. I HEARD MANY THINGS IN HELL.

AM I MAD? **HA!** OBSERVE HOW CALMLY I CAN TELL YOU THE WHOLE STORY.

IT IS IMPOSSIBLE TO SAY HOW THE IDEA FIRST ENTERED MY BRAIN. I LOVED THE OLD MAN. HE HAD NEVER WRONGED ME. I HAD NO DESIRE FOR HIS MONEY. YET THE IDEA HAUNTED ME DAY AND NIGHT. I THINK IT WAS HIS **EYE**... YES, IT WAS THIS!

THE CLASSIC TALE BY
EDGAR ALLAN POE
AS INTERPRETED BY
RONN SUTTON
COLOR BY BENJAMIN WRIGHT

ONE OF HIS EYES RESEMBLED THAT OF A *VULTURE* — A PALE BLUE EYE WITH A FILM OVER IT. WHENEVER IT FELL UPON ME MY BLOOD RAN COLD! SO I MADE UP MY MIND TO TAKE THE LIFE OF THE OLD MAN, AND THUS RID MYSELF OF THE EYE FOREVER.

YOU FANCY ME MAD. BUT YOU SHOULD HAVE SEEN HOW WISELY I PROCEEDED — WITH WHAT CAUTION AND FORESIGHT I WENT TO WORK! I WAS NEVER KINDER TO THE OLD MAN THAN DURING THE WEEK BEFORE I KILLED HIM.

EVERY NIGHT ABOUT MIDNIGHT I TURNED THE LATCH OF HIS DOOR AND OPENED IT — OH, SO GENTLY! I PUT IN A LANTERN, THEN THRUST IN MY HEAD. OH, HOW CUNNINGLY I MOVED!

I WENT VERY SLOWLY, SO THAT I MIGHT NOT DISTURB THE OLD MAN'S SLEEP. I COULD SEE HIM AS HE LAY UPON HIS BED. WOULD A *MADMAN* HAVE BEEN SO WISE AS THIS?

I UNDID THE DOOR ONLY SO MUCH THAT JUST A SINGLE THIN RAY FELL UPON THE VULTURE EYE. I DID THIS EVERY NIGHT AT MIDNIGHT, FOR SEVEN LONG NIGHTS.

BUT I FOUND THE EYE ALWAYS CLOSED, SO IT WAS IMPOSSIBLE TO DO THE DEED. FOR IT WAS NOT THE OLD MAN WHO VEXED ME — IT WAS HIS *EVIL EYE*.

EVERY FOLLOWING MORNING I GREETED HIM BOLDLY, INQUIRING HOW HE HAD PASSED THE NIGHT.

BY THE EIGHTH NIGHT I COULD SCARCELY CONTAIN MY FEELINGS OF TRIUMPH. I CHUCKLED TO THINK THAT THE OLD MAN COULD NOT DREAM OF MY SECRET DEEDS OR THOUGHTS.

AND PERHAPS HE HEARD ME, FOR HE SPRANG UP IN THE BED, CRYING OUT, *"WHO'S THERE?"* BUT I KNEW THAT HE COULD NOT SEE THE OPENING OF THE DOOR IN THE DARK.

I KEPT QUITE STILL AND SAID NOTHING. FOR A WHOLE HOUR I DID NOT MOVE A MUSCLE, AS I DID NOT HEAR HIM LIE DOWN. HE WAS STILL SITTING UP IN THE BED, LISTENING.

PRESENTLY, I HEARD A GROAN OF MORTAL TERROR. I KNEW WHAT THE OLD MAN FELT. HE HAD BEEN LYING AWAKE EVER SINCE THE FIRST PREMONITION, AND HIS FEARS HAD BEEN GROWING UPON HIM SINCE. DEATH'S BLACK SHADOW HAD ENVELOPED ITS VICTIM. IT WAS WHAT CAUSED HIM TO FEEL MY PRESENCE WITHIN THE ROOM.

WHEN I HAD WAITED A LONG TIME, I RESOLVED TO TURN ON THE LANTERN. A SINGLE DIM RAY, LIKE THE THREAD OF A SPIDER, SHOT OUT AND FELL UPON THE VULTURE EYE.

IT WAS OPEN — *WIDE, WIDE OPEN* — AND I GREW FURIOUS AS I GAZED UPON IT; A DULL BLUE WITH A HIDEOUS VEIL OVER IT THAT CHILLED THE VERY MARROW IN MY BONES.

THEN THERE CAME TO MY EARS A LOW, DULL, QUICK SOUND. IT WAS THE BEATING OF THE OLD MAN'S *HEART*, AND IT ONLY INCREASED MY FURY.

I SCARCELY BREATHED. I HELD THE LANTERN MOTIONLESS, BUT THE HELLISH TATTOO OF THE HEART INCREASED. IT GREW QUICKER AND LOUDER EVERY INSTANT. THE OLD MAN'S TERROR MUST HAVE BEEN EXTREME! THE SOUND GREW *LOUDER*, I SAY, LOUDER EVERY *MOMENT!*

TH-THUMP!

TH-TH

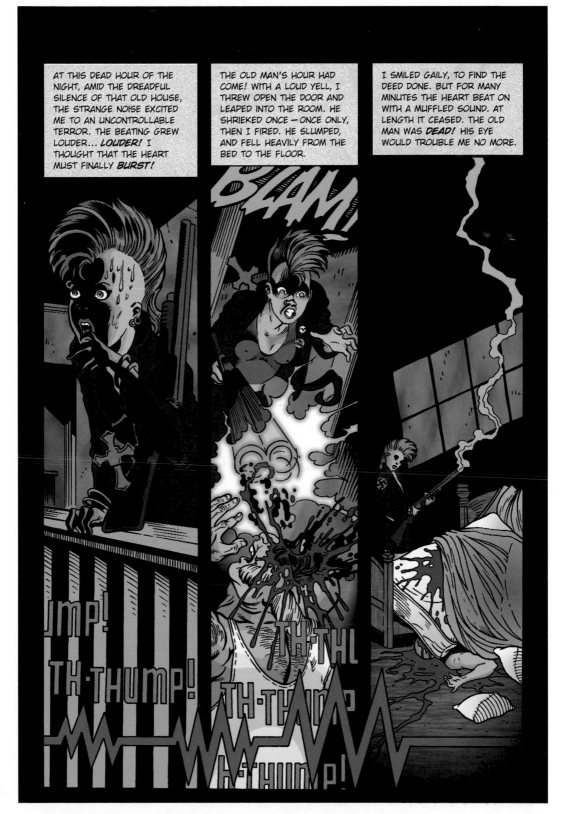

AT THIS DEAD HOUR OF THE NIGHT, AMID THE DREADFUL SILENCE OF THAT OLD HOUSE, THE STRANGE NOISE EXCITED ME TO AN UNCONTROLLABLE TERROR. THE BEATING GREW LOUDER... *LOUDER!* I THOUGHT THAT THE HEART MUST FINALLY *BURST!*

THE OLD MAN'S HOUR HAD COME! WITH A LOUD YELL, I THREW OPEN THE DOOR AND LEAPED INTO THE ROOM. HE SHRIEKED ONCE — ONCE ONLY, THEN I FIRED. HE SLUMPED, AND FELL HEAVILY FROM THE BED TO THE FLOOR.

I SMILED GAILY, TO FIND THE DEED DONE. BUT FOR MANY MINUTES THE HEART BEAT ON WITH A MUFFLED SOUND. AT LENGTH IT CEASED. THE OLD MAN WAS *DEAD!* HIS EYE WOULD TROUBLE ME NO MORE.

IF **STILL** YOU THINK ME MAD, CONSIDER THE WISE PRECAUTIONS I TOOK FOR THE CONCEALMENT OF THE BODY. AS THE NIGHT WANED, I WORKED HASTILY, BUT IN SILENCE.

I FIRST DISMEMBERED THE CORPSE, THEN I TOOK UP THREE PLANKS FROM THE FLOOR AND DEPOSITED ALL WITHIN.

I REPLACED THE BOARDS SO CLEVERLY, SO CUNNINGLY, THAT NO **HUMAN** EYE — NOT EVEN HIS **EVIL EYE** — COULD HAVE DETECTED ANYTHING WRONG. THERE WAS NO BLOOD-STAIN OR EVIDENCE OF ANY KIND REMAINING. I HAD BEEN TOO CAREFUL FOR THAT.

WHEN I HAD MADE AN END OF THESE LABORS, IT WAS FOUR O'CLOCK. THEN THERE CAME A KNOCK AT THE DOOR.

THERE ENTERED THREE MEN; OFFICERS OF THE POLICE. A SHRIEK HAD BEEN HEARD BY A NEIGHBOR DURING THE NIGHT, AND THE OFFICERS HAD BEEN SENT TO SEARCH THE PREMISES.

I SMILED — WHAT HAD I TO FEAR? I BADE THE GENTLEMEN WELCOME. THE SHRIEK, I EXPLAINED, WAS MY OWN IN A DREAM. THE OLD MAN, I SAID, WAS AWAY IN THE COUNTRY.

I BADE MY VISITORS SEARCH THE HOUSE. I LED THEM, AT LENGTH, TO HIS CHAMBER. THERE I SHOWED THEM HIS TREASURES, SECURE AND UNDISTURBED. IN THE AUDACITY OF MY TRIUMPH, I SAT UPON THE VERY SPOT BENEATH WHICH REPOSED THE CORPSE OF THE VICTIM.

THE OFFICERS WERE SATISFIED. MY MANNER HAD CONVINCED THEM. THEY SAT AND I ANSWERED CHEERILY AS THEY CHATTED. BUT ERE LONG, I WISHED THEM GONE. MY HEAD ACHED, AND I FANCIED A RINGING IN MY EARS. IT BECAME MORE DISTINCT, AND I FOUND THAT THE NOISE WAS NOT *WITHIN* MY EARS.

NO DOUBT I GREW VERY PALE AS THE SOUND INCREASED. I GASPED FOR BREATH, AND YET THE OFFICERS HEARD NOTHING. I AROSE AND I TALKED MORE VEHEMENTLY, WITH A HEIGHTENED VOICE, BUT *STILL* THE NOISE STEADILY INCREASED.

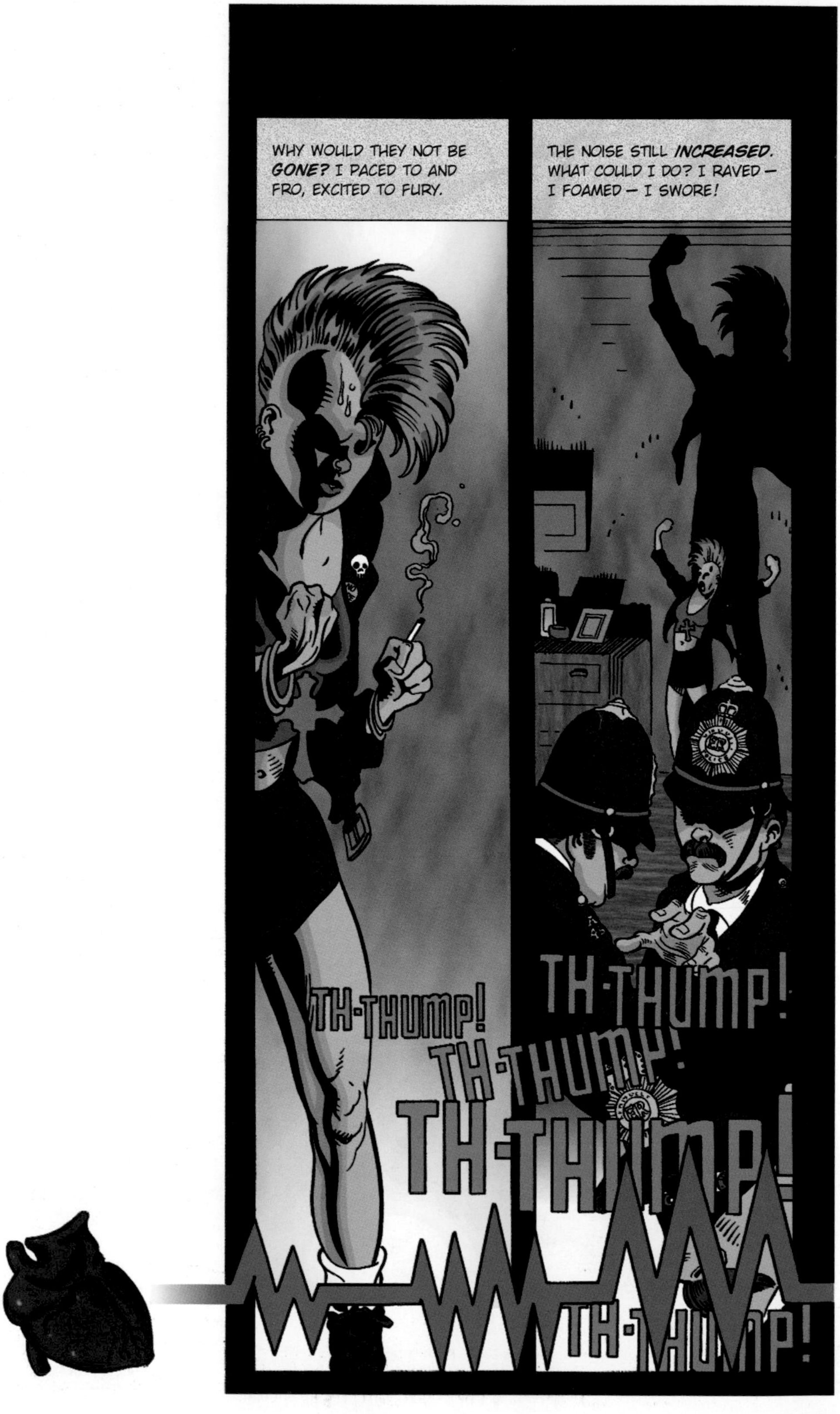
WHY WOULD THEY NOT BE GONE? I PACED TO AND FRO, EXCITED TO FURY.
THE NOISE STILL INCREASED. WHAT COULD I DO? I RAVED — I FOAMED — I SWORE!
TH-THUMP!
TH-THUMP!
TH-THUMP!
TH-THUMP!
TH-THUMP!

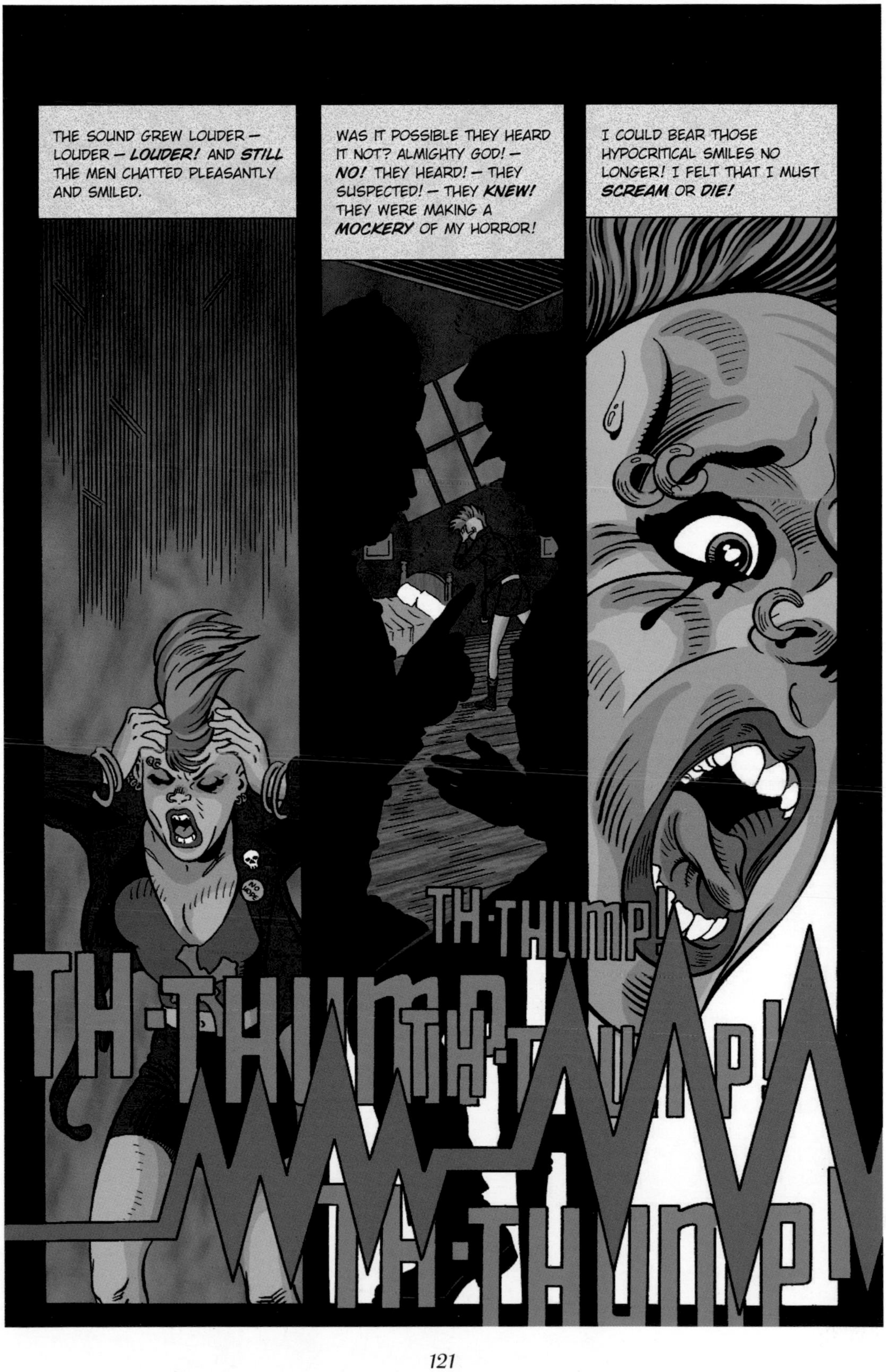
THE SOUND GREW LOUDER — LOUDER — LOUDER! AND STILL THE MEN CHATTED PLEASANTLY AND SMILED.
WAS IT POSSIBLE THEY HEARD IT NOT? ALMIGHTY GOD! — NO! THEY HEARD! — THEY SUSPECTED! — THEY KNEW! THEY WERE MAKING A MOCKERY OF MY HORROR!
I COULD BEAR THOSE HYPOCRITICAL SMILES NO LONGER! I FELT THAT I MUST SCREAM OR DIE!
TH-THUMP!
TH-THUMP!
TH-THUMP!
TH-THUMP!

"*VILLAINS!*" I SHRIEKED, "DISSEMBLE NO MORE! I *ADMIT* THE DEED! — HERE, *HERE!* — IT IS THE *BEATING* OF HIS *HIDEOUS HEART!*"

End.

The "Red Death" had long devastated the country.

No pestilence had ever been so fatal, or so hideous. Blood was its Avatar and its seal—the redness and the horror of blood.

There were sharp pains, and sudden dizziness, and then profuse bleeding at the pores, with dissolution. The scarlet stains upon the body and especially upon the face of the victim shut him out from the aid and from the sympathy of his fellow-men.

And the whole seizure, progress and termination of the disease, were the incidents of half an hour.

the Masque of the Red Death

by Edgar Allan Poe, adapted by Stan Shaw

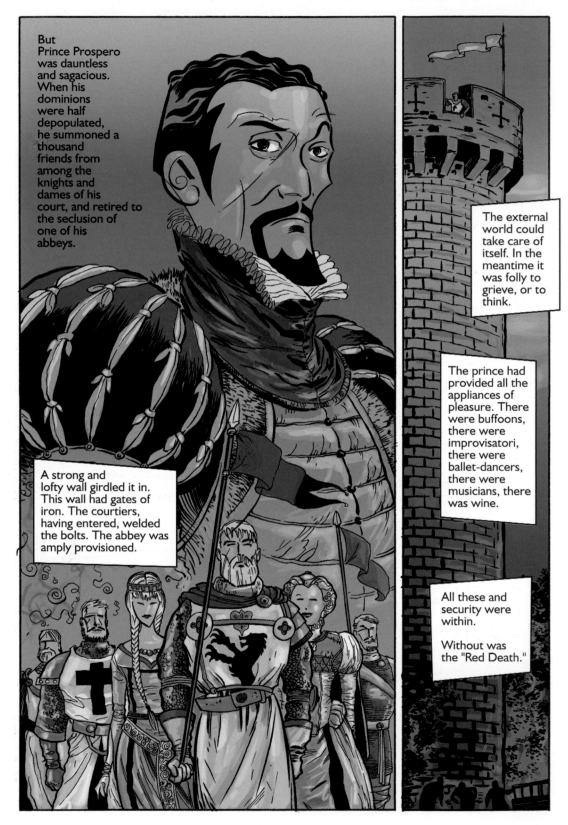

But Prince Prospero was dauntless and sagacious. When his dominions were half depopulated, he summoned a thousand friends from among the knights and dames of his court, and retired to the seclusion of one of his abbeys.

A strong and lofty wall girdled it in. This wall had gates of iron. The courtiers, having entered, welded the bolts. The abbey was amply provisioned.

The external world could take care of itself. In the meantime it was folly to grieve, or to think.

The prince had provided all the appliances of pleasure. There were buffoons, there were improvisatori, there were ballet-dancers, there were musicians, there was wine.

All these and security were within.

Without was the "Red Death."

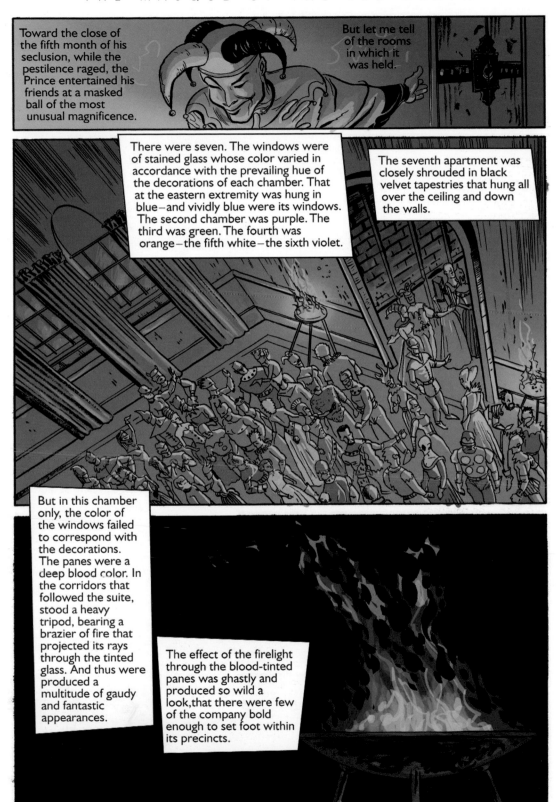

Toward the close of the fifth month of his seclusion, while the pestilence raged, the Prince entertained his friends at a masked ball of the most unusual magnificence.

But let me tell of the rooms in which it was held.

There were seven. The windows were of stained glass whose color varied in accordance with the prevailing hue of the decorations of each chamber. That at the eastern extremity was hung in blue—and vividly blue were its windows. The second chamber was purple. The third was green. The fourth was orange—the fifth white—the sixth violet.

The seventh apartment was closely shrouded in black velvet tapestries that hung all over the ceiling and down the walls.

But in this chamber only, the color of the windows failed to correspond with the decorations. The panes were a deep blood color. In the corridors that followed the suite, stood a heavy tripod, bearing a brazier of fire that projected its rays through the tinted glass. And thus were produced a multitude of gaudy and fantastic appearances.

The effect of the firelight through the blood-tinted panes was ghastly and produced so wild a look, that there were few of the company bold enough to set foot within its precincts.

It was in this apartment that there stood a gigantic clock of ebony. Its pendulum swung to and fro with a heavy, monotonous clang; and at each lapse of an hour there came from the brazen lungs of the clock a sound which was of so peculiar a note that the musicians were constrained to pause in their performance.

The waltzers ceased their revolutions, and there was a brief disconcert of the whole gay company; and, while the chimes rang, it was observed that even the giddiest grew pale.

But when the echoes had ceased, a light laughter at once pervaded the assembly, and the musicians looked at each other and smiled as if at their own nervousness and folly.

Then, after the lapse of sixty minutes, there came yet another chiming of the clock, and the same disconcert.

XII

126

In spite of these things, it was a gay and magnificent revel. There were much glare and glitter and piquancy and phantasm.

There was much of the beautiful, much of the wanton,

much of the bizarre, something of the terrible,

and not a little of that which might have excited disgust.

Excepting the black seventh chamber, the apartments were crowded, and in them beat feverishly the heart of life. And the revel went whirlingly on,

until there commenced the sounding of midnight upon the clock.

Then the music ceased; the evolutions of the waltzers were quieted; and there was an uneasy cessation of all things as before. But now there were twelve strokes to be sounded by the clock; and thus it happened, perhaps, that more of thought crept into the meditations of the revellers.

And thus, too, it happened, perhaps, that before the last echoes of the last chime had sunk into silence, there were many who had become aware of the presence of a masked figure which had arrested no attention before.

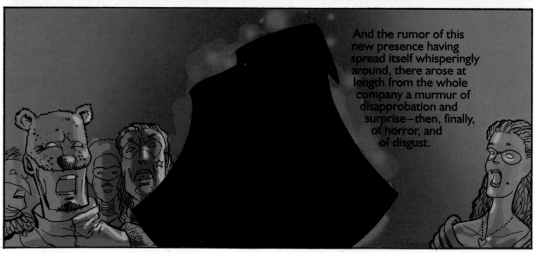

And the rumor of this new presence having spread itself whisperingly around, there arose at length from the whole company a murmur of disapprobation and surprise—then, finally, of horror, and of disgust.

In an assembly of phantasms such as I have painted, it may well be supposed that no ordinary appearance could have excited such sensation. In truth the masquerade license of the night was nearly unlimited; but the figure in question had gone beyond the bounds of even the prince's indefinite decorum.

The figure was tall and gaunt, and shrouded from head to foot in the habiliments of the grave. Its mask was made to resemble the countenance of a stiffened corpse. And yet all this might have been endured by the mad revellers. But the mummer had gone so far as to assume the type of the Red Death. His vesture was dabbled in blood—and his broad brow was besprinkled with the scarlet horror.

When the eyes of Prince Prospero fell upon this spectral image, his brow reddened with rage.

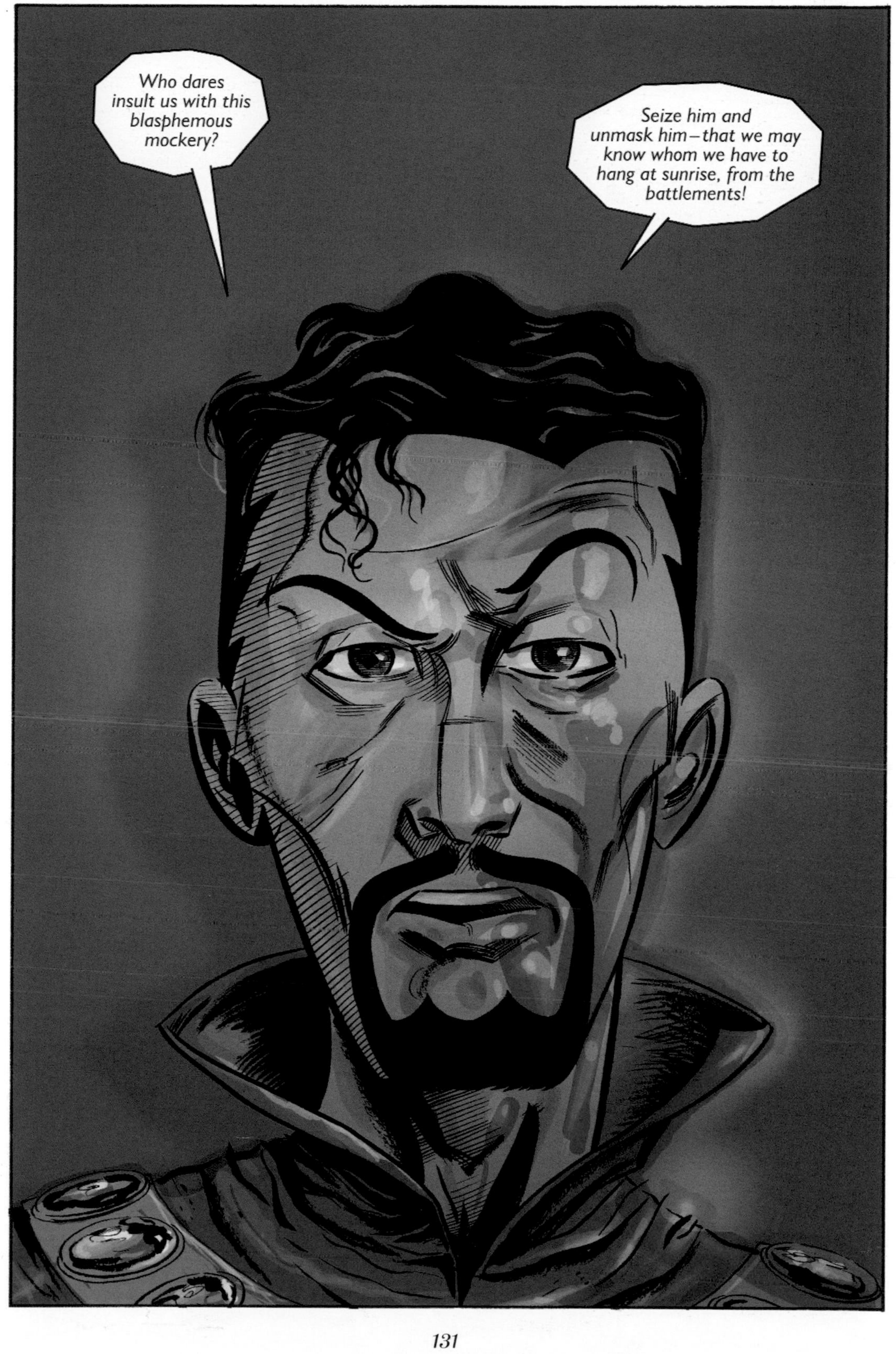
Who dares insult us with this blasphemous mockery?
Seize him and unmask him–that we may know whom we have to hang at sunrise, from the battlements!

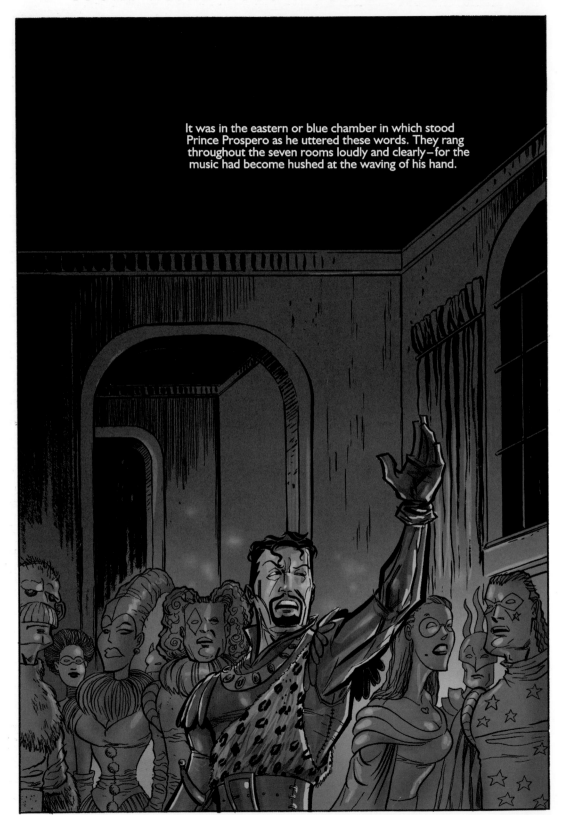

It was in the eastern or blue chamber in which stood
Prince Prospero as he uttered these words. They rang
throughout the seven rooms loudly and clearly—for the
music had become hushed at the waving of his hand.

As the prince spoke, the intruder was near at hand, and with deliberate and stately step, he made closer approach to the speaker. None put forth hand to seize him; unimpeded, he passed within a yard of the prince;

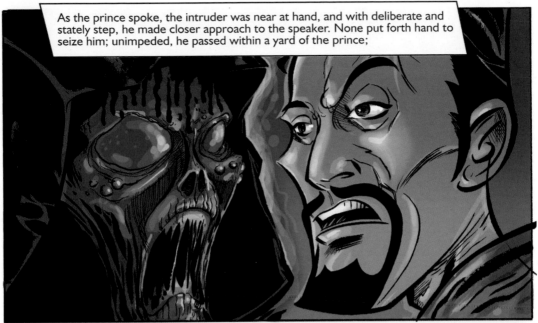

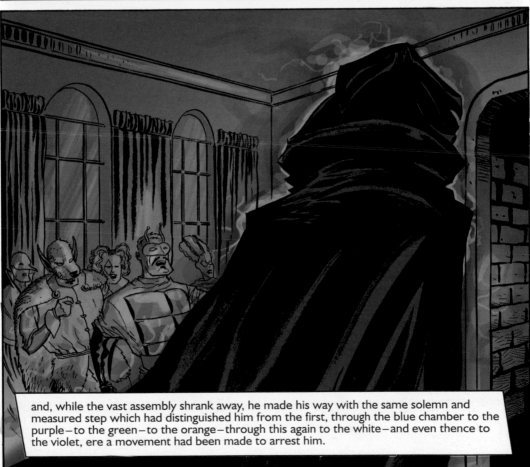

and, while the vast assembly shrank away, he made his way with the same solemn and measured step which had distinguished him from the first, through the blue chamber to the purple—to the green—to the orange—through this again to the white—and even thence to the violet, ere a movement had been made to arrest him.

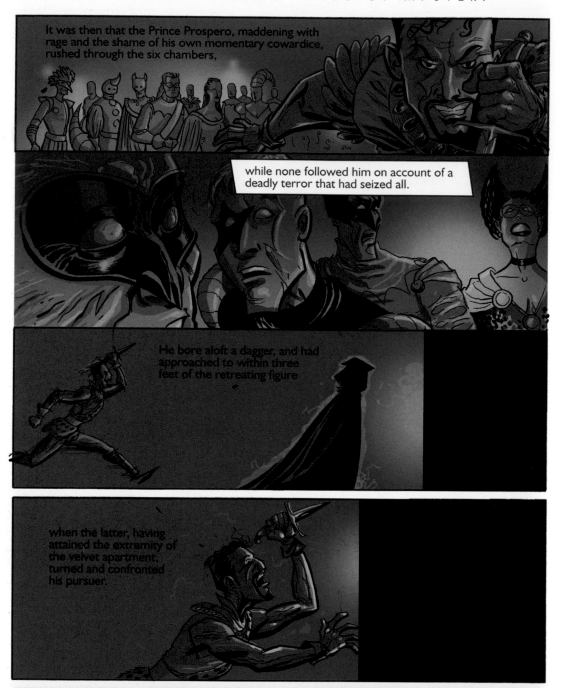

It was then that the Prince Prospero, maddening with rage and the shame of his own momentary cowardice, rushed through the six chambers,

while none followed him on account of a deadly terror that had seized all.

He bore aloft a dagger, and had approached to within three feet of the retreating figure

when the latter, having attained the extremity of the velvet apartment, turned and confronted his pursuer.

There was a sharp cry – and the dagger dropped upon the sable carpet, upon which, instantly afterwards, fell prostrate in death the Prince Prospero.

Summoning the wild courage of despair, a throng of the revellers threw themselves into the black apartment,

and, seizing the mummer, within the shadow of the ebony clock,

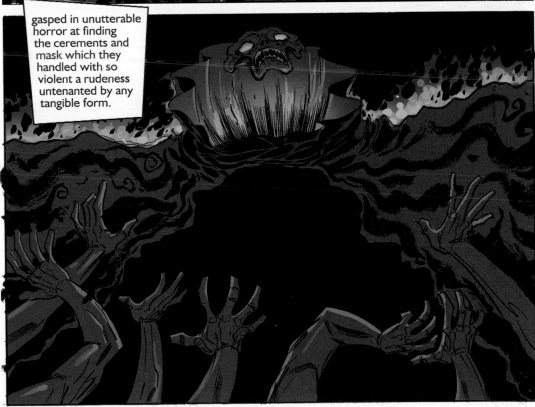

gasped in unutterable horror at finding the cerements and mask which they handled with so violent a rudeness untenanted by any tangible form.

135

And now was acknowledged the presence of the Red Death. He had come like a thief in the night.

And one by one dropped the revellers in the blood-bedewed halls, and died each in the despairing posture of his fall. And the life of the ebony clock went out with that of the last of the gay.

And the flames of the tripods expired.

And Darkness and Decay and the Red Death held illimitable dominion over all.

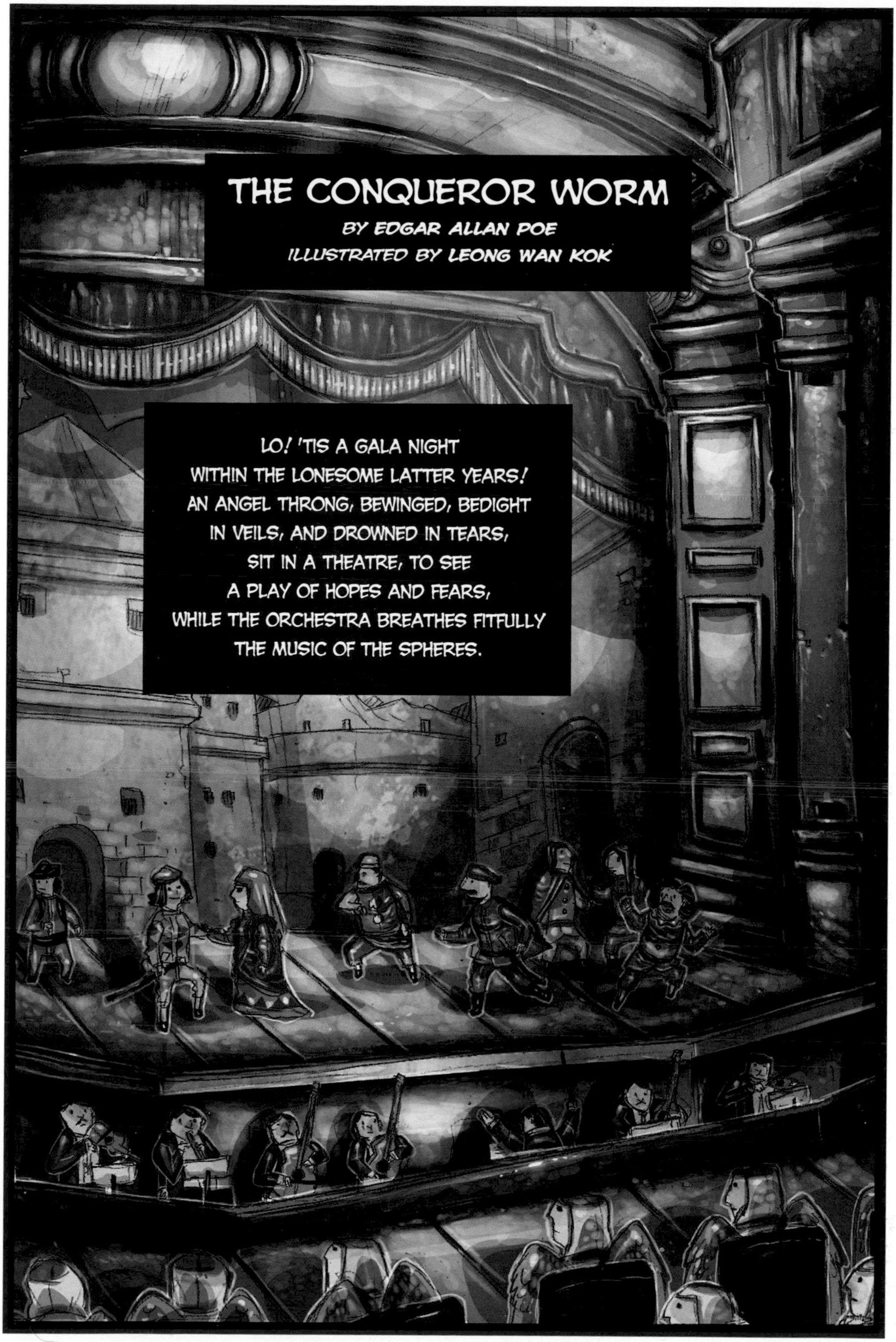
THE CONQUEROR WORM
BY EDGAR ALLAN POE
ILLUSTRATED BY LEONG WAN KOK
LO! 'TIS A GALA NIGHT
WITHIN THE LONESOME LATTER YEARS!
AN ANGEL THRONG, BEWINGED, BEDIGHT
IN VEILS, AND DROWNED IN TEARS,
SIT IN A THEATRE, TO SEE
A PLAY OF HOPES AND FEARS,
WHILE THE ORCHESTRA BREATHES FITFULLY
THE MUSIC OF THE SPHERES.

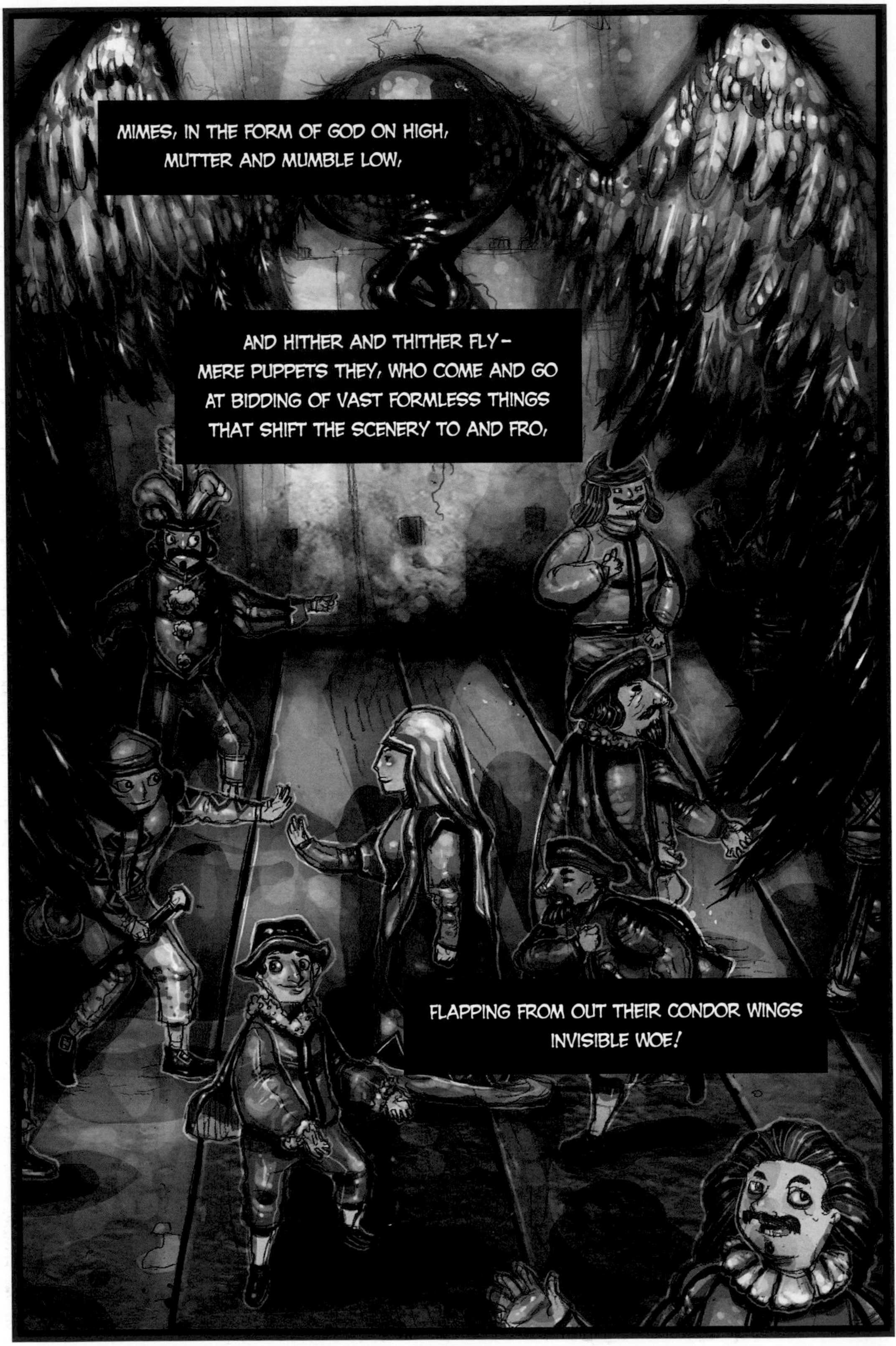
MIMES, IN THE FORM OF GOD ON HIGH,
MUTTER AND MUMBLE LOW,
AND HITHER AND THITHER FLY–
MERE PUPPETS THEY, WHO COME AND GO
AT BIDDING OF VAST FORMLESS THINGS
THAT SHIFT THE SCENERY TO AND FRO,
FLAPPING FROM OUT THEIR CONDOR WINGS
INVISIBLE WOE!

THAT MOTLEY DRAMA – OH, BE SURE
IT SHALL NOT BE FORGOT!

WITH ITS PHANTOM CHASED FOR EVERMORE,
BY A CROWD THAT SEIZE IT NOT,

THROUGH A CIRCLE THAT EVER RETURNETH IN
TO THE SELF-SAME SPOT,
AND MUCH OF MADNESS, AND MORE OF SIN,
AND HORROR THE SOUL OF THE PLOT.

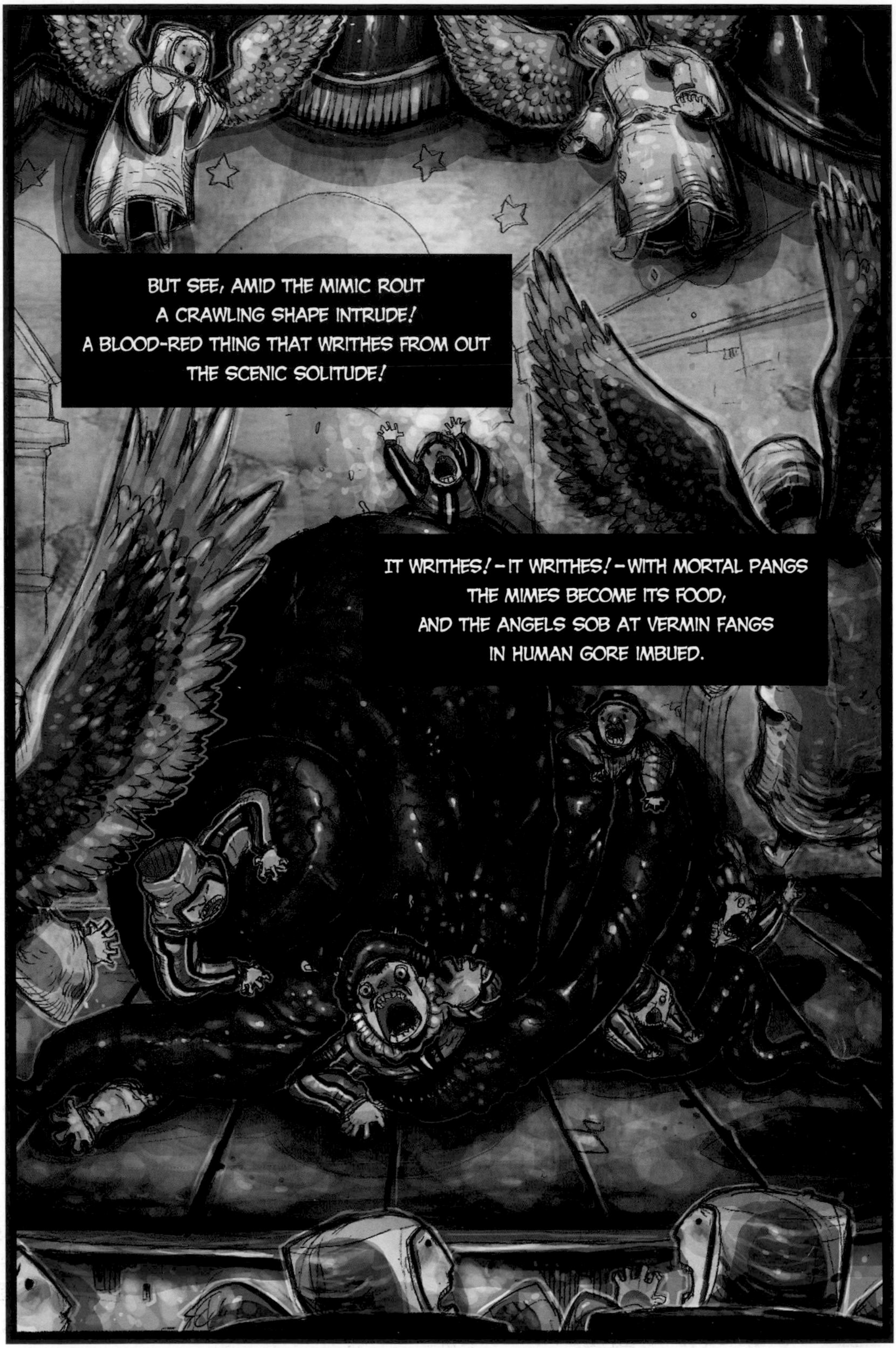
BUT SEE, AMID THE MIMIC ROUT
A CRAWLING SHAPE INTRUDE!
A BLOOD-RED THING THAT WRITHES FROM OUT
THE SCENIC SOLITUDE!
IT WRITHES! – IT WRITHES! – WITH MORTAL PANGS
THE MIMES BECOME ITS FOOD,
AND THE ANGELS SOB AT VERMIN FANGS
IN HUMAN GORE IMBUED.

OUT—OUT ARE THE LIGHTS—OUT ALL!
AND, OVER EACH QUIVERING FORM,
THE CURTAIN, A FUNERAL PALL,
COMES DOWN WITH THE RUSH OF A STORM,

AND THE ANGELS, ALL PALLID AND WAN,
UPRISING, UNVEILING, AFFIRM

THAT THE PLAY IS THE TRAGEDY, "MAN,"
AND ITS HERO THE CONQUEROR WORM.

EDGAR ALLAN POE

Edgar Allan Poe, one of America's greatest writers, was the orphaned son of itinerant actors, and led a tumultuous adolescence of drink and gambling, which resulted in the failure of both his university and military careers. Throughout his life he was plagued by poverty, poor health, insecurity, and depression, much by his own doing and a result of his continuing problems with alcohol. He struggled unsuccessfully as a writer until winning a short story contest in 1833. Poe's subsequent writing ranged from his rigorously metrical poetry to short stories, from journalism and distinguished literary criticism to the pseudo-scientific essays of *Eureka*. Today he is generally acknowledged as the inventor of both the gothic short story and the detective story, a pioneer of early science fiction and the founding father of the horror genre. He rightfully occupies the first volume in the *Graphic Classics* series, and more stories by Edgar Allan Poe appear in:

Graphic Classics: Edgar Allan Poe
Horror Classics: Graphic Classics Volume 10
Gothic Classics: Graphic Classics Volume 14

MICHAEL MANNING *(cover, page 30)*

Michael is an illustrator, animator, tattoo designer and comics artist. His artwork has been exhibited in galleries and museums internationally, including San Francisco's prestigious Yerba Buena Center for the Arts. Manning's best known works include *The Spider Garden* and *Tranceptor* graphic novel series (NBM Publishing) and the art collection *Inamorata* (Last Gasp). Born in New york City, Manning studied Film and Animation at Boston's School of the Museum of Fine Arts. He eceived the 2008 Garland Award for Best Multimedia/Digital Design for his anime-style projection sequences for the techno-opera *Paradise Lost: Shadows & Wings*. A California resident since 1991, Manning currently lives and works in downtown Los Angeles. More of his artwork can be seen online at www.thespidergarden.net and in the pages of:

Graphic Classics: Edgar Allan Poe
Graphic Classics: Robert Louis Stevenson
Graphic Classics: Bram Stoker
Horror Classics: Graphic Classics Volume 10
Adventure Classics: Graphic Classics Volume 12

SKOT OLSEN *(page 1)*

While growing up in Connecticut, Skot and his parents spent their summers sailing up and down the coast of New England and all over the West Indies. It was on these long trips that he developed his love for the sea which forms the basis for much of his work. A graduate of the Joe Kubert School of Cartoon and Graphic Art, Skot now lives on the edge of the Florida Everglades, where he concentrates on paintings which have been featured in numerous publications and exhibited in galleries in Florida, New York and California. A large collection of his work is online at www.skotolsen.com and in:

Graphic Classics: H. P. Lovecraft
Graphic Classics: Bram Stoker
Adventure Classics: Graphic Classics Volume 12
Fantasy Classics: Graphic Classics Volume 15

MAXON CRUMB *(page 2)*

Maxon will be familiar to many readers from his appearance in Terry Zwigoff's 1994 award-winning film, *Crumb*. (If you have not seen this amazingly frank and honest documentary, go rent the DVD immediately.)

While brother Robert's work may be more well-known, Maxon is equally talented as both a writer and artist. His gritty fantasy story, "Stigmata," appears in *Crumb Family Comics* (1998, Last Gasp). He illustrated *Maxon's Poe* (1997, Cottage Classics), and in 2001 created an illustrated novel called *Hardcore Mother* (CityZen Books.) More amazing illustrations by Maxon can be found in:

Graphic Classics: H. P. Lovecraft
Graphic Classics: Bram Stoker
Graphic Classics: Robert Louis Stevenson

ANTONELLA CAPUTO *(page 4, 96)*

Antonella Caputo was born and raised in Rome, Italy, and now lives in Lancaster, England. She has been an architect, archaeologist, art restorer, photographer, calligrapher, interior designer, theater designer, actress and theater director. Her first published work was *Casa Montesi*, a fortnightly comic strip which appeared in the national magazine *Il Giornalino*. She has since written ten comedies for children and scripts for comics and magazines in the UK, Europe and the US Antonella works with Nick Miller as the writer for Team Sputnik, and has collaborated with Nick and others in:

Graphic Classics: Arthur Conan Doyle
Graphic Classics: H.G. Wells
Graphic Classics: Jack London
Graphic Classics: Ambrose Bierce
Graphic Classics: Mark Twain
Graphic Classics: O. Henry
Graphic Classics: Rafael Sabatini
Graphic Classics: Oscar Wilde
Graphic Classics: Louisa May Alcott
Graphic Classics: Special Edition
Horror Classics: Graphic Classics Volume 10
Adventure Classics: Graphic Classics Volume 12
Gothic Classics: Graphic Classics Volume 14
Fantasy Classics: Graphic Classics Volume 15

RENO MANIQUIS *(page 4)*

Reno has been writing and illustrating short stories for comics in the Philippines since age thirteen. During his college days, he created the newspaper strip *Maskarado* and in the late '90s he revived the character as a self-published comic book. He has contributed to various publications in the Philippines, including the award-winning anthology *Siglo: Passion, Colors Magazine* in Europe, and independent publications in the US including *Stormblazer, Sequential Suicide: Slop, The Hierograph,* and *Wall of Angels*. He has also published *Tabloid Komiks,* an anthology which showcases stories and art from Filipino creators. Reno is also a professional graphic designer, and is currently a regular artist for Moonstone Books, where he has worked on characters including *The Phantom, Captain Action, Lady Action,* and *Domino Lady*. You can find his work online at www.capsulezone.tk and renomaniquis.co.cc. Reno's stories can be seen in:

Graphic Classics: Ambrose Bierce
Western Classics: Graphic Classics Volume 20

MOLLY KIELY *(page 29)*

Molly Kiely is a Canadian artist best known for her *Diary of a Dominatrix* comics series and the graphic novels *That Kind of Girl* and *Tecopa Jane*, all published by Fantagraphics. Molly currently lives in Tucson, Arizona, where she does art and chases her toddler, Perla, around the house. She maintains a journal at www.mollykiely.com and her artwork can be seen at

www.tecopajane.com. Molly's work also appears in
Graphic Classics: Oscar Wilde
Gothic Classics: Graphic Classics Volume 14

NEALE BLANDEN (page 42)
Neale was born in 1963 in Melbourne, Australia, and started self-publishing in 1988 under the monicker "Beautiful Artform." He has published sixteen comics to date, and has appeared in anthologies in Australia, Canada, Europe and the US. He is also an animator, and teaches classes in cartooning. His artwork has been exhibited in galleries in Australia, Canada and Europe. Neale is currently working on two books, one a compilation of past work, and one of new material. Neale's comics are included in
Graphic Classics: Ambrose Bierce
Graphic Classics: Robert Louis Stevenson

NELSON EVERGREEN (page 44)
Nelson Evergreen lives on the south coast of the UK with his partner and their imaginary cat. A busy freelance illustrator, in his spare time he can be found working on any one of a number of comic strips featuring his inventions *Shadowquake & Shnookie*, *Mark E. Moon*, and *Edith Rock & Hilda Roll*. On top of this he's hard at work writing and illustrating *Roof Monsters* — a children's picture book/graphic novel hybrid — and slowly piecing together a collection of absurd short stories provisionally titled *The Bearded Hover-Pig and Other Nonsenses*. The card acompanying *Christmas Classics* was Nelson's first work for *Graphic Classics*, and "Berenice" was his first story contribution. See more of Nelson's art at www.nelson-evergreen.com.

ROGER LANGRIDGE (page 56)
New Zealand-born artist Roger Langridge is the creator of Fred the Clown, whose online comics appear at www.hotelfred.com. Fred also shows up in print in *Fred the Clown* comics. With his brother Andrew, Roger's first comics series was *Zoot!* published in 1988 and recently reissued as *Zoot Suite*. Other titles followed, including *Knuckles*, *The Malevolent Nun* and *Art d'Ecco*. Roger's work has also appeared in numerous magazines in Britain, the US, France and Japan, including *Deadline*, *Judge Dredd*, *Heavy Metal*, *Comic Afternoon*, *Gross Point* and *Batman: Legends of the Dark Knight*. Roger now lives in London, where he divides his time between comics, children's books and commercial illustration. See more comics by Roger in:
Graphic Classics: Edgar Allan Poe
Graphic Classics: Arthur Conan Doyle
Graphic Classics: Jack London
Graphic Classics: Ambrose Bierce
Graphic Classics: Robert Louis Stevenson
Graphic Classics: Rafael Sabatini
Science Fiction Classics: Graphic Classics Volume 17

ROD LOTT (page 58)
Oklahoma City resident Rod Lott is a corporate managing editor for a media company. He is the founder and editor of *Bookgasm*, a daily book review and news site at www.bookgasm.com, and for twelve years he published the magazine *Hitch: The Journal of Pop Culture Absurdity*. Rod's humorous essays have been published in several anthologies, including *May Contain Nuts* and *101 Damnations*. You can find more comics adaptations by Rod in:
Graphic Classics: Edgar Allan Poe
Graphic Classics: Arthur Conan Doyle

Graphic Classics: H.G. Wells
Graphic Classics: H.P. Lovecraft
Graphic Classics: Jack London
Graphic Classics: Ambrose Bierce
Graphic Classics: O. Henry
Graphic Classics: Rafael Sabatini
Graphic Classics: Louisa May Alcott
Horror Classics: Graphic Classics Volume 10
Adventure Classics: Graphic Classics Volume 12
Gothic Classics: Graphic Classics Volume 14
Fantasy Classics: Graphic Classics Volume 15
Western Classics: Graphic Classics Volume 20

LISA K. WEBER (page 58)
Lisa K. Weber is an artist currently residing in Brooklyn, New York, having graduated from Parsons School of Design in 2000 with a BFA in Illustration. Her whimsically twisted characters and illustrations have appeared in various print, animation, and design projects including work for clients *Scholastic*, *Cricket Magazine*, Children's Television Workshop, and many others. Her work is featured in a series of young reader's books, called *The Sisters Eight*, published by Houghton Mifflin in 2009. She has also participated in exhibitions in New York and Philadelphia. To see more of her art, visit www.creatureco.com. Lisa has provided comics and illustrations for:
Graphic Classics: H.P. Lovecraft
Graphic Classics: Ambrose Bierce
Graphic Classics: Mark Twain
Graphic Classics: O. Henry
Graphic Classics: Oscar Wilde
Graphic Classics: Louisa May Alcott
Gothic Classics: Graphic Classics Volume 14

CRAIG WILSON (page 76)
A director/storyboard artist of animation and an illustrator, Craig Wilson has been pushing a pencil professionally for over twenty years. Craig lives in Vancouver, Canada. You can see more of his work on his blog at www.money-shotz.blogspot.com or his website at www.boardguy.ca. "The Oval Portrait" is Craig's first project for *Graphic Classics*. You can find an alternate version of the story illustrated by Leong Wan Kok in *Gothic Classics*.

RICH RAINEY (page 80)
A ghostwriter who also writes about ghosts, Rich Rainey's nonfiction books include *Phantom Forces* (a history of warfare and the occult), *Haunted History*, and *The Monster Factory*, a book about classic horror writers and the real-life incidents that inspired their fiction. He's written more than thirty adventure and science fiction novels and also created *The Protector* series about a modern day D'Artagnan in New York City. His short fiction has appeared in literary and mystery magazines and numerous anthologies, including *Best Detective Stories of the Year*. In the comics field he created *Flesh Crawlers* for Kitchen Sink, *Antrax: One Nation Underground* for Caliber, and has written for *The Punisher* and Neil Gaiman's *Lady Justice*. Rich also adapted stories for:
Graphic Classics: H.P. Lovecraft
Graphic Classics: Bram Stoker
Graphic Classics: Oscar Wilde
Graphic Classics: Louisa May Alcott
Christmas Classics: Graphic Classics Volume 19
Western Classics: Graphic Classics Volume 20

BRAD TEARE (page 80)

Utah artist Brad Teare maintains a career as both an illustrator and a fine arts painter and woodcut artist. Clients include *The New York Times*, *Fortune* and Random House, where he illustrated for authors such as James Michener, Ann Tyler, and Alice Walker. Teare's comics creations have appeared in *Heavy Metal* magazine and the *Big Book* series from Paradox Press. He is the author of the graphic novel *Cypher* from Peregrine Smith Books (excerpted in *Rosebud 20*). *Cypher* is also available for the Amazon Kindle via Brad's blog at sandhogcomics.blogspot.com. More of his work can be viewed online at www.officialcypherfansite.com and at www.bradteare.com. Brad's stories appear in:

Graphic Classics: H.G. Wells
Fantasy Classics: Graphic Classics Volume 15
Science Fiction Classics: Graphic Classics Volume 17

ANDY EWEN (page 94)

Andy's illustrations have appeared in *The Progressive*, *Isthmus*, and *The New York Times Book Review*. He was the featured artist in *Rosebud 10* in 1997 and has contributed many illustrations to the magazine since, including a series in *Rosebud 22*. Andy confesses to a "lifelong obsession with human mortality." His personal, dreamlike drawings add a new dimension to Poe's "Spirits of the Dead." In addition to his ability as a graphic artist, Ewen is also a talented musician. For more than twenty-five years he has been singer, guitarist and songwriter for Honor Among Thieves, one of the Madison, WI area's most respected bands.

BENJAMIN WRIGHT (page 94, 113)

Benjamin wears many hats — in addition to being a colorist, he's a graphic designer, writer, and illustrator. He's worked on tabletop roleplaying games (*Cyberpunk*, *Cybergeneration*, *Mekton Z*, *Bubblegum Crisis*, *VOTOMs*,) manga (*Naruto*, *Yu-Gi-Oh!*, *Bleach*, *Pokémon*, *Gundam*,) magazines (*Shonen Jump*, *Wizard*, *ToyFare*, *Anime Insider*, *Otaku USA*, *Animerica*) and t-shirts. Born and raised in New York City, Benjamin now lives and works in San Francisco. For *Graphic Classics* he's colored stories in:

Christmas Classics: Graphic Classics Volume 19
Western Classics: Graphic Classics Volume 20

ANTON EMDIN (page 96)

"Sailing his drawing board in a sea of India ink," Anton produces illustrations and comic art for a variety of books, magazines, websites and advertising agencies, both in Australia (where he resides) and internationally. Aside from the necessary commercial work, Anton contributes his weirdo comic art to underground comix anthologies, both in Australia and overseas, as well as self-publishing his own mini-comic, *Cruel World*. You can find his work at www.antongraphics.com, and in:

Graphic Classics: Ambrose Bierce
Graphic Classics: Robert Louis Stevenson
Christmas Classics: Graphic Classics Volume 19

GLENN SMITH (page 96)

Glenn "Glenno" Smith is an old mate of Anton Emdin and an art mercenary of some reknown in his native Australia. Mainly concerning himself with illustrating for bands these days, he's occasionally coaxed out of his comfort zone to do comics again. You will find him rockin' out in new band[...] through www.glennoart.co[...] Pest" is Glenn's first contri[...]

RONN SUTTON (page 113)

Canadian artist Ronn Sutton continues to strive to be an "overnight success" after several decades of drawing comics. He has drawn probably close to 200 comic book stories, working for a variety of publishers including a nine year stint of drawing *Elvira, Mistress of the Dark* for Claypool Comics. Many of these were written by his longtime love, Janet L. Hetherington. Sutton's first published comics go back to the early 1970s and he has drawn horror, romance, adventure, science fiction and humor comics (as well as comics based on *The Man From UNCLE*, Sherlock Holmes, Vampira and others). For seven years he also did freelance courtroom sketches for newspapers and tv, including the trial of Momin Khawaja, the first man in Canada convicted of terrorism. He recently drew a series of *Honey West* comics based on the 1960s books and tv series starring the late Anne Francis. "The Tell-Tale Heart" is Sutton's first work for *Graphic Classics*. See more of his art at www.ronnsutton.com.

STAN SHAW (page 123, back cover)

Stan Shaw illustrates for various clients all over the country including *The Village Voice*, *Esquire*, *Slate*, Starbucks, The Seattle Mariners, Nintendo, Rhino Records, Microsoft, BET, POV, DC Comics, ABC-NEWS.com, Wizards of The Coast, *Amazing Stories*, *Vibe*, The Flying Karamazov Brothers and *Willamette Week*. In addition to practicing illustration, Stan teaches it, at Cornish School of the Arts, School of Visual Concepts and Pacific Lutheran University. He is now part of a group of artists advising on an illustration textbook. His work can be seen at www.drawstanley.com. Stan has illustrated stories in:

Graphic Classics: Ambrose Bierce
Graphic Classics: O. Henry
Graphic Classics: Rafael Sabatini
Graphic Classics: Oscar Wilde

LEONG WAN KOK (page 137)

Leong Wan Kok, known to Malaysian comic readers as Puyuh, was born in Malaysia in the year of the rabbit. He now lives in Kuala Lumpur. He has been active in the comics industry in Malaysia since 2002, when he was invited to represent his country in the "Asia in Comics" festival in Tokyo. His alternate version of "The Oval Portrait," in *Gothic Classics*, was his first work published in the US. In December 2006, his book of illustrations and comics, *Astro Cityzen*, was released in Malaysia, and in 2010 the hardcover collection *Twisted Mind of 1000 Tentacles*. You can see more of Leong Wan Kok's work online at www.1000tentacles.com and in:

Gothic Classics: Graphic Classics Volume 14
Fantasy Classics: Graphic Classics Volume 15

TOM POMPLUN

The designer, editor and publisher of *Graphic Classics*, Tom also designed *Rosebud*, a journal of fiction, poetry and illustration, from 1993 to 2003, and in 2001 he founded *Graphic Classics*. Tom is currently co-editing *African-American Classics* with artist Lance Tooks. This 22nd volume in the *Graphic Classics* series will present stories and poems by early Black American writers, including Paul Laurence Dunbar, Jean Toomer, W.E.B. Du Bois, Langston Hughes, Charles W. Chesnutt and [...] interpreted by contemporary [...] nd illustrators. Look for it in